The Door

Creative Writing Anthology #1

Buckinghamshire
New University
http://www.bucks.ac.uk

With Contributions from:

Laura Bonfield,
Gráinne C. Byrne,
Sophie Dale,
Suzanne Harbour,
P. T. Holmes,
Ben Hopkins,
Samuel Long,
Rory Kenny,
Allen Stroud
& Thomas Whylie

The Door: Creative Writing Anthology #1.
First published in the UK in 2016 by: HWS PRESS &
BUCKINGHAMSHIRE NEW UNIVERSITY
ISBN: 978-1-910987-98-8

Contents

Introduction

Welcome to the first story anthology produced by students of Buckinghamshire New University's BA (Hons) Creative Writing for Publication course.

This collection of short stories and poetry is the work of our first year of students, starting the course in September 2015. Many of these works were assignments begun at the start of the year and refined through peer editing and feedback from lecturers on the course.

This anthology epitomises the new philosophy of the degree. Creative writing assignments are not drafted, marked and forgotten. Instead, each are refined and improved through subsequent drafts and feedback from students and staff right up until the end of the year.

Each cohort aims their work towards a publication. This helps focus everyone towards a deadline. Additionally, students are taught the skills to produce their own ebook and print copy master.

During my time as a writer I spent long periods trying to make my work better, refining, improving, tweaking, eventually to the point that I lost track of what was better and what was worse. Having other writers around me, understanding what was good advice and what was just a series of platitudes, seeing where I was going wrong, took time and only happened when I made myself vulnerable, sharing my work, making mistakes, accepting them and getting better.

This collection of stories is a step on a longer journey. Enjoy them for what they are; for some, their first publications, for others a new achievement for their portfolios. With this collection, each writer is moving towards where they are going and what they want to achieve.

Allen Stroud.

Broken Shells
by Suzanne Harbour

I tiptoe down the garden path and turn to check the kitchen window one last time to make sure no one is watching. The hinges of the door shriek as I pull it open, and something thumps behind my ribs as I step inside.

"The Anderson shelter is not a playroom," Mother always says.

I know that, really. It's dark and cramped in here and smells like fear. But it has the same pull as a ghost story: you know it's scary, but you just have to hear it anyway.

I drag my stool over to the small table and sit the doll Jimmy gave me on the seat next to me. I'm not really a doll person, but Jimmy says I need to play more like a girl to keep Mother happy while he's gone.

I pick up the teapot, which has a cozy with the oddest pattern: swirling browns and oranges that always makes me think of autumn. I pretend to pour my doll some tea.

"Would you like a biscuit, Maddie?"

I make my doll's head nod and wish I really did have some biscuits. We are too short on butter to make any at the moment, so Mother says.

I wonder what Charlie would think if he could see me now, playing tea parties like a silly little girl, and I feel my cheeks colour.

I hear Mother calling my name, thank goodness. This game was boring and I didn't do it right. All I really want to do is kick a ball and run so fast my legs burn.

I leave the doll behind and walk slowly back to the house, because I don't want *this* tea time to come.

My older brother, Jimmy, ruffles my hair. "I won't be gone for long, kiddo."

I don't even look at him as I take my seat at the kitchen table next to my younger brother, Stewie. I don't want him to go, I don't, I don't!

"Kitty, elbows off the table," Mother says.

I sit back in my chair and fold my arms across my chest. Mother exhales, sharply. "Kitty, don't slouch!"

I roll my eyes and Jimmy tries not to laugh. I'm going to miss him so much, my only friend in this house.

Father comes in and sits at the head of the table. Mother places the pot of stew – potato and vegetable again – in front of him to dish up. Jimmy, not Father, gets the largest portion this time.

"Not sure when you'll get a decent meal again," Father says to him, and silence falls on us like a heavy blanket.

I wouldn't really call the meal decent. Hot and filling, yes, but I am so sick of potatoes. We all scrape at our bowls and drink our water, and even Jimmy can't seem to make his usual jokes.

Father sits back in his chair and wipes his mouth with a napkin. "All packed then, Jimmy?"

Jimmy nods. "Yes Father, I'm all ready to go."

"We're mighty proud of you, son. You've taken the call like a man." He clears his throat. Does he have a cold, or is something choking him?

And I can't believe what he just said. Like a man? But Jimmy is just… Jimmy! He's too young for war, that's what I want to shout out. You need to keep your trap shut, Father always says. I'm trying, I really am. I ball up my fists and stick them under my legs, thinking this might help me keep quiet.

When the sun sets, we draw the blackout blinds. We live on the outskirts of London, but Father says there's no need for us to evacuate, because our Anderson shelter is so strong. He's a carpenter and built it himself, adding lots of unnecessary details – Mother tells me.

We spend the rest of our evening together sitting around the little table to play snakes and ladders. We act like a happy little family, with pretend smiles and jokes. No-one wants to talk about tomorrow.

"Kitty, Stewart, time for bed," Father says.

"But, Father…" I begin to protest.

"No arguments." The stern look on his face stops me whinging.

I plod to the sitting room door, give one last look at Jimmy and head towards my room.

After I have brushed my teeth and slipped into my nighty, I grab my statue of Mary and kneel beside my bed. I put my hands together and squeeze my eyes shut.

"Dear Mary…"

I pause, stumbling at the first prayer line. Do I pray to Mary, God or Jesus? I'm always confused by this, because everyone always uses a different name. Jesus is the son of God and Mary, I know that. But no-one's really explained this; does that mean Mary was married to God? Because I thought she was married to Joseph. They should make these things clearer.

"Dear Mary, God, Jesus… and Joseph," I say, to be on the safe side. "It's me, Kitty. I know I don't pray much, but please can you look after my brother, Jimmy? And my family? Oh, and end the war. Amen."

I'm not sure if that's how I'm meant to pray. At church, it's all Hail Mary's and Our Father's. I know those prayers off by heart, but it doesn't feel like they would work for Jimmy because the words are all wrong. I've always told Mother that I say my prayers every night, like a good Catholic girl should. I never do, it's all a lie.

As I climb into bed, I remember some of the things I heard at church about prayer. If you don't ask you don't get – I think that's the rule. So I'll pray, every day now, because my brother's life depends on it.

The weeks are dragging by. Charlie is best at keeping my mind off things, but the evenings are getting dark now, so there's less time for football. We have to squeeze it in when we can, but Mother's so distracted that at least it's easy to sneak off.

I pull open the front door. Charlie stands there, wearing his funny, wonky grin. He needs a haircut. His scruffy curls are hanging too long.

"Kitty, come on," he says. "We're all waiting for you."

I put my fingers to my lips. "Shhh!" I turn around to check that Mother isn't nearby. "Where are we playing?"

"On the street."

I huff. "Charlie, Mother will see me. Can't we play somewhere else?"

"Stop worrying. I bet she won't even notice. Come on." He grabs my hand and drags me out the doorway.

"Okay, I'm coming," I say, pulling free and shutting the door as softly as I can.

Tony has already picked the teams, and I'm glad to be on Charlie's. I'm the best footballer on the street. It's funny how that makes me unpopular with both the boys and girls, though for completely different reasons. All except Charlie, of course.

After scoring three goals and heading towards my fourth, Tony manages to tackle me. I fall to the ground, my face skidding across the gritty road, and know I'm not going to be able to hide this from Mother.

"Foul!" Charlie shouts. He reaches out a hand and I shrug him off. Then my ankle gives, and I have no choice but to let him help me.

"Wasn't a foul, was it lads?" Tony glares at his friends, then me.

"It was." Charlie looks around the crowd for support, but everyone seems suddenly interested in their shoes or the pavement. I want to punch Tony in his smug little face, but Charlie's grip is tight and I can feel something hot and sticky trickle down my face.

"We should go inside," I mumble.

Charlie takes me towards his house instead of mine. I give Tony one last look, hoping that he can read what my face is saying – *I will get you back*. He laughs and walks away.

My ankle isn't so bad and the cuts aren't deep, but that doesn't save me from being in trouble when I get home.

"Kitty, what on earth happened?" Mother asks as soon as I enter the house.

"I fell," I mumble and look away.

"She fell playing football," Stewie says.

I glare at him. "Traitor!" I hiss.

"Kitty! Football!" And Mother is off on her usual rantings, throwing her arms wildly as she talks. "…And not a care about your brother…"

She means Jimmy. He's always been the golden boy. Stewie is their beloved 'baby'. Me, I'm just the one who gets in the way. A disappointment at every turn, Mother always says.

"… he's risking his life for his country, and you go flouting yours willy nilly!"

It's all a bit over the top, but that doesn't stop it upsetting me. We haven't had a letter from Jimmy in weeks.

It's gone quiet, and Mother is looking at me with an eyebrow raised. Maybe she asked a question, but I stopped listening a while ago.

"Sorry?" I say, and it doesn't really sound like I am.

Mother makes a curt nod. "As you should be. Now, get your shoes gleaming." She hands me polish and a cloth. "And I mean gleaming."

I plop off my chair and go into the kitchen with the polish. I take my shoes off and my heart sinks: they are scuffed too badly to be fixed, and Mother must have known it.

When my hands are hot and sore from the rubbing, Mother finally turns from the dishes and says, "That'll do."

I put my shoes away without speaking to her and run upstairs to my room. Grabbing my pen and paper, I write another letter to Jimmy, moaning about Mother. He would understand my upset: he was the one who taught me to play football and cricket and helped me keep everything a secret. I read back over my letter and then screw it up into a ball. Maybe it would all seem a bit silly to him and he had enough to worry about. I start the letter again, and talk about nothing important.

When I'm done, I kneel by my bed with my Mary statue and squeeze my eyes shut – my daily ritual. I never miss a prayer anymore, because I worry what would happen if I did.

"Dear Mary, God, Jesus and Joseph. Please keep Jimmy safe. Please let him write us a letter. And keep my mother safe and …" I use my fingers to count off my family members and friends who I pray for every day.

I know my prayers are keeping them safe because my Sunday school teacher said, "You reap what you sow." I didn't get it at first, but I think she meant if I don't pray and people get hurt, then it's my fault. Yes, I'm pretty sure that's it.

"…And, if you're not too busy, can you make Mother less boring and send a plague of boils to Tony? Amen."

It's funny how telegrams are both good and bad. They're kind of like a lucky dip at the fayre – you never know what you're going to get until you open it.

We were lucky. It looks like Mary, God, Jesus or Joseph has waved their wand and granted my wish. My prayers have kept us all safe, and Jimmy's coming home tomorrow. But I'll keep praying, until this war is over, because all our lives depend on it.

"Dear Mary, God, Jesus and Joseph. Please keep Jimmy safe…"

"Kitty, look!" Stewie calls from my doorway.

"Urgh, go away, Stewie!"

He's waving an envelope and hoping on the spot. "But it's a letter for you. Mother just found it under a hat in the hallway. Must have been there days!"

"Give it!" I snatch it out of his hand and slam the door in his face.

"Aww, let me see it!"

I hear his muffled whine, but ignore him as I sit on my bed with the letter. It's from Jimmy. I read it and re-read it over and over until my eyes sting too much to stay open.

"Kitty, hurry up!" Charlie says.

He's at the door keeping a lookout while I rummage under Jimmy's bed.

"Just another minute," I say as I slither forwards.

I move another box and see the treasure I've been searching for. I grab the plimsolls, still caked in dried mud that make them smell of mould, and shuffle myself backwards.

"Let's go!" I say, waving the plimsolls in front of Charlie's face.

We tiptoe down the stairs. The kitchen door is shut, so we leave the house without Mother's nagging and run out to the street.

Jimmy's old shoes are two sizes too big, but a balled-up sock at the toes helps to make them fit better. I wish I'd found his letter days ago, then I'd have had the plimsolls longer. But he's home today, and that's all that matters.

The match begins, and I score a goal within minutes. Girls can't kick, run or throw, so they say. Girls are meant to sew, bake and play with dolls. But here I am, better at sport than any boy and the worst baker on the street.

"Kitty!"

Mother stands at the doorway of our house, wearing her apron and a scowl as she calls my name. She's been a lot jollier since the telegram arrived, but I know I'm in trouble now. I say goodbye to Charlie and run towards her, praying she doesn't notice my feet. It wasn't stealing, because Jimmy said I could have them. I even have the letter in my pocket to prove it.

"No more football!" The pulsing vein in her forehead distracts me. I sometimes worry it might explode and shower me with blood. "You promised that you would help me in the kitchen today. Jimmy will be home later."

I nod and follow her inside. I feel too happy about Jimmy to protest or make an excuse.

I stand next to Mother, watching her crack the egg on the side of the cup. She pulls the shell apart and pours the egg between each half, her movements so elegant. I watch the clear liquid stuff trickle neatly into the cup, leaving the yolk behind in the shell.

"Never let a speck of yolk enter the white," she says. "That's the secret to the perfect meringue."

I wonder who made the first ever meringue. Who decided to whip up egg whites with sugar? It's an odd thing to decide to do, and I'm pretty sure I'll never master it.

Mother holds an egg out to me. "Your turn."

My eyes widen. I take it and stare blankly at the cup. I crack it on the side and pull the shell apart, then tip the sticky, gooey contents from one half of shell to the other. A blob of that white stuff escapes, splatting onto the table. I try to save the rest, but the jagged edge of the shell stabs the yolk: I watch it run down my fingers.

Mother sighs. "Kitty." She says my name like a telling off. I have tried to use the same tone with Stewie, but never seem able to get it right.

"I'm sorry," I mumble.

She quickly scoops the egg into another cup, muttering under her breath, "That'll be your tea tonight then."

We only have two eggs left from our ration, so Mother takes over. She begins whisking the whites. "Can you weigh out the sugar? It's in the cupboard."

I get the sugar and then weigh it out. "Mother, there isn't enough."

She looks at the scales, frowning. "We only need a little more. There should be some in the shelter."

I grab a torch and skip towards our Anderson shelter. I clamber inside, feeling the door swing shut behind me. My torch is the only source of light, so it takes me a while to find the sugar. I should head straight back, but I can't resist reading the letter again. I pull it out of my pocket and take a seat next to the doll Jimmy gave me.

"Hey kiddo,

You've probably already seen the telegram, and the letter to our parents, so you'll know I'm coming home soon. I hope you haven't been too worried. I probably won't be able to play football with you for a while, so you'll have to keep practising with the boys on the street. I meant to give you my old plimsolls before I left, but I guess I forgot. They're under my bed, if you want them.

There are whispers that war will be over soon, sis. Not long now, and our lives will be back to normal. I can't wait to see you all. Keep safe.

Lots of love,

Jimmy."

I smile as I re-read the letter again. I don't know when exactly the war will end, but I know for certain now that my family will be safe. I just want everything back to normal.

I feel the ground shake before I even hear the explosion. Knocked off my feet, I lose my torch and everything goes pitch black.

I curl up into a ball, and then something lands on me. It's heavy, it hurts and I can't move my legs. I think that's my doll lying in front of my face, all dusty, trapped and alone. Like me. I don't get it. There wasn't a siren, no warning at all. Where were my family now, and my friends on the street? And why hadn't my prayers worked this time?

My stomach turns and I feel sick as I remember last night. Stewie interrupted me as I said my prayers, and I didn't bother to finish them off: I only prayed for Jimmy.

I reach for Maddie and pull her to my chest: my only link with Jimmy, my only reminder of my family as I realise the truth.

I did this.

Tempest
by Sophie Dale

The storm is coming. I can feel it.

Emotion trickles down my face the way the rain rips across the window. Outside, I see an unsettling vision of London. The landmarks are crumbling, the strength of the buildings weakens with age, demanding something visceral to arise in their place. The Tower of London pleads for forgiveness; I watch it cling to the solid ground below. The past haunts that dreadful place. It knows its fate is imminent, but hopes it will escape. The home of death in London still believes in second chances. A place is ruined through history and rebuilds, conquers its fears, but the name remains tainted to its memory. Or maybe what truly deserves to die still lingers in the deserted halls of the Tower.

I can imagine being on the brink of dying, terrified and alone only to look up into the eyes of the devil himself. The power and strength of the storm, its fate, is forcing the evil to suffer its own creation: fear.

What hope do I have if this tempest defeats evil itself?

Hope. Really, what is it? This substance, this belief I'm blinded by. It is invisible; this philosophical treasure, begging a certain question to be answered. Why is there something rather than nothing? There is always something, love or hope or a blinding light inside them to do good. Why do we believe in such notions that the human mind has made up only centuries before? But this is the last bit of scientific magic I have left. Against all odds, above all else, I believe there is always hope. Now and forever. I will not surrender.

Then there is *her*. She lingers around me like mist in a forest and yet she's the closest thing I have to family. I don't understand why, she's beautiful and what every other guy is after and, well, I'm not. But something has occurred to me. She is showing signs of something I can't quite recognise. Her torture and constant shadow is a blessing, she says, that best friend you just can't escape. Lately, she's become more immature and playful than usual. What once was my invincible anchor, now crumbling and mouldering. The fragments are floating to the surface for only my eyes to piece together.

Yet I still depend on her.

I love her.

She's tearing and scraping away at me, she speaks notions about angels and demons and more specifically the "truth of our God."

My parents, they believed in such theories. Theories that lead them to believe that science was flawed. They were Christians, and God was, well, God. What else could possibly compete? You'd think flesh and blood was more important than their unfathomable connection with the "All Father". Not even their love for me, their daughter, could compete. I wanted them for me so I exploded with a million different emotions and went too far. A flash of light and that was it, they were gone.

My stability is in peril. I can feel shift and so can she.

She calls me an angel, like one with long, majestic, feathery, white wings; she says they're invisible to mundane eyes. I argue that I can't see them and she just tells me to wait.

Who am I?

I don't know because sometimes I'm surprised by what I can do, these things that no one else can do. Not even her. It's like I'm making myself up as I go along. And throughout all this, I bless the broken road behind me that brought me this far and lead me to her.

She's like oxygen, I need her to breathe.

The point still stands; she's beginning to act a little more out of place than usual. She's telling of war and the oncoming storm and I can't help but fear it, the vision of it.

She says I will have to pick a side, not that I even know the choices. Is it World War Three?

The only answer I ever get from her is that the mundane lives here have lost all faith, and in that loss, they no longer know who to fear.

I don't want to be feared. I've always seen myself as good. I am good.

I read about insane people. I observe them on television, I cannot be a replica of my parents, but she could be. I am good, right?

Her storm keeps trying to rage itself into my life, she's acting juvenile, condescending, toying around with my mind. She says God is gone, she thinks she has a way of finding him. I tell her not to bother. Hard to imagine how God would even dream of helping me. I establish the courage for myself, I need no help. Not from the supposed "All Mighty" at least.

She knows me, she knew my parents. She was there through it all and now what? Why does she torture me with these unearthly questions? Join the heavenly war… what is she talking about? We give each other strength to succeed; they said history had a tendency to repeat itself.

But she's here now, in my room.

She always carries a diary with her, and the name at the top in big letters reads: 'LUCY.' Shaking, I look to her, in the scared way I only know how, I don't know this person, no one can just appear in a room without using a door; I don't understand. I can't understand. I won't understand until she tells me what's going on, I am not fit for war.

"You are my weapon," she says with grace.

"I am no weapon," I repeat over and over, until I'm blue in the face.

She comes very close, I can feel her breath on my neck as she whispers in my ear. "You're an angel of the heavens."

There wasn't much I could muster to that. "You're crazy!" I reply with a giggle.

She mimics my laughter. She grabs me and we vanish.

Suddenly, we're flying, wait, no, not flying; we're falling. And as we fall, the wind is tearing apart my face and all I can taste in my mouth is the constant screaming. How did we get in the sky? Why does she want to kill me?

Wait, I've been here once before, yes, falling. It is then the memories come flooding back. Crash landing by a magnificent oak tree, alone in a field of nothingness. But I am nothingness no more, and as I rise without a scratch, the shackles of the mundane disintegrate.

Cast from the heavens, nineteen years ago, memories of my entire heavenly existence erased, until now. Lucy has rescued me from my ignorant prison.

Then all at once, it finally occurs to me. All the signs fit together. her appearance changes. "You are Satan in the flesh."

"Oh, that's a little harsh; I much prefer Lucy in this body."

"What do you want, Lucy?"

"God has left you. The angels cast you out like they did to me. I think you deserve some vengeance for the millennia of scrutiny they forced upon you. You have hope, right? For a better world? Well this is what I'm offering you right now. You're a fallen angel, I'm a fallen angel, we are the same."

The words melt from her mouth as if she'd been planning them for her entire imprisoned existence. And they meld with me as if I've believed them all this time. I repeat, "We *are* the same."

Then in a second we're plucked from the sky and into the white room.

This is the angels' interrogation room – the most feared room of all the worlds. Not even hell can live up to it; how the blinding light raises you in its harsh majesty, only to make you face yourself as imperfect and unworthy, condemned to self torment and despair.

Lucy is with me, tied down by the symbols that no angel can escape unless broken by another. We face each other and around us I see the glinting weapons. Then in a flash, a face appears in the room, one I never thought I would see, never remembered until now. His dark hair, blue eyes, still mesmerising and in an instant I remembered what it felt like to love him.

"Michael?"

He turns to me and smiles the same little smile as before, but his eyes are blank. He doesn't know me like this. He gazes at Lucy. What am I thinking? Angel and human love are two different things, where the latter is much more powerful, human love can cause quakes and destroy worlds; or so I've heard. Now I've seen such love and want it even more here, with Michael.

How could he bear to look at me bound like this if he recognised me? Our love was refuted but I wouldn't dare think he would hurt me. The trouble is, though, he doesn't know me in this body. What are the chances of him believing a stranger?

He picks up the angel blade and presses it to Lucy's abdomen. The flesh parts as he draws the weapon back in a straight line. I shut my eyes against the sight. Even though she is Lucifer, I still feel something for her, for what she did. The angel blade is the only thing that can truly kill us; even its simple graze from its razor sharp edge causes enormous pain.

This wound does not disappoint as Lucy cries out, but quickly master's herself. "The storm is coming. I can feel it. Michael, brother, your delusion is your flaw," she gasps. "You had a woman that loved you and a life you could have lived but you let God control you and yet, where is he?"

Michael stares at her, the blade hanging loosely in his hand.

"Where is God?" Lucy repeats, trying to provoke a response.

"This is pointless," Michael says. "You cannot shake my faith." There is anger in his words. I had hoped never to hear that again.

"Oh, has Daddy gone missing?" Lucy mocks.

Michael turns to me as Lucy spirals into fake loud laughter.

"So, who are you and why did you make the mistake of hanging out with Lucifer?"

I remembered my name even as he asks for it. "I am Adriel and I was cast away from the hea—"

His hands are on me. "Is it really you?" he demands. "It can't be, I would know. Adriel has been gone for almost two decades."

"A blink of an eye. Look at me, my body is nineteen years of age, but I remember everything from before. You can't resist all that you don't believe."

"Please, tell me I'm imagining this?"

"You're not; I was kicked out because I caused so much destruction."

"I know what you did."

Those words penetrate. Michael's smile is gone. Lucy speaks up then, still cackling at the scenario she's just created.

"Dear big brother, the first angels to feel love and then pulled apart, I feel so special."

"Don't mock us," Michael warns. "She's here because of you and she was taken away because of you too."

The direction of my life has always been decided by others; I remember now. Lucy came to me before, but in her true form, not this girlish shell. She offered the same vengeance when I was unsure. I caused death and destruction amongst the heavens, determined to lure God out. But he did not come; our father remained on his unknown perch watching us or not for all we knew. Eventually, the anger and destruction became addictive, drowning my regret in self-justification for my actions.

God does not care anymore. And then it all dawns on me, this is a civil war, angel pitted against angel to fight for what's right; free will or control by the one who created us and abandoned us.

But my regret is still there and my mind is not yet made up.

"Adriel, you belong up here, with me."

Lucy lets out a dry heaving noise.

"Adriel," Michael takes hold of my bound face and looks into my eyes. "You need to understand what a mistake it would be to choose this. If you go, I can't save you. Stay, and this war doesn't need to happen."

Lucy opens her mouth, but Michael is by her side and ties a rope between her teeth. "Shush brother, you've had nineteen years with her, I wish to get a word in." Michael turns to me once more. "I know I haven't always been there for you—"

"You left me on Earth with no memories, ignorant and alone. You may as well have shot me in the heart. I was unprotected, Michael. You hear me, All Father? I was vulnerable, unknowingly powerful and anyone of the millions of monster and demons could've murdered me and then what would you have done?"

"It wasn't what I wanted."

"The storm is getting closer and closer, Michael. You can't stop this war. This is a gospel for all us fallen angels, you can't understand what I need to do. You are respected and loved, I am not. Don't make me do something I'll regret. I love you, crazy or not, this love will never die, but I will fight for what needs to happen whether that is with Lucy or on my own."

Michael's expression clouds, his mouth sets into a grim line. He picks up the angel blade and holds it quivering below my chin. He's close now, so close.

I've always seen myself as good. I am good. I'm just a fallen angel that knows what she wants after all her life of living a lie.

"You are my light, Michael," I tell him. "Without you, there was an awful lot of darkness on Earth, but it was Lucy that found me and she rescued me, not you and I cannot forgive you for that."

For a moment, he looks hurt. Then Lucy's unbearable cackle echoes around the room. He turns towards her. The angel blade in his hand.

I'm aware of another presence in the room. A new voice, one I don't recognise speaks. "We need information."

"I'm in the middle of the interrogation." Michael says.

"Look me in the face, have some respect."

"I'm an Archangel, I owe you no respect, I've lived longer than you, since before the beginning of time and yet you make me pay *you* respect? You don't know what I can do."

Suddenly, Lucy is free. The angel blade is plucked from Michael's hands and buried in the chest of the stranger. He didn't see it coming, I didn't see it coming. As the light flares from his eyes his invisible wings become visible and catch fire. It's beautiful to watch them blaze and burn, I almost miss doing such things, I miss being the Angel of Death.

I glance at Michael. He has broken the seal the holds us here. He moves towards me, unbinding me from the symbolic ropes. "Run!" he says. "Run as fast as you can and don't look back."

"Thank you, brother, I'll forgive the torture and not kill you," Lucy says. She grabs my arm. The flash of light is so blinding I have to cover my eyes.

We're back on Earth. No? We're in Hell.

"We have to prepare for the angels."

I'm aware of what happened, but a bit confused as to why we need to prepare now. Lucy sees my lack of urgency to get ready and shakes me.

"I killed Zachariel, he's judge, jury and executioner upstairs so they're going to be pretty annoyed."

"Just us two though?"

"Oh honey, I've been recruiting people since before your second birth, this has been a plan in the making for centuries, and I thought you knew that?"

"It seems my memory is still a little bit spotty from the twenty years I spent as a mundane."

"Well suit up, it's time to call on our friends."

In that moment, Lucy stands and sends out a message to those on our side and I hear it.

"Brothers and sisters, the time has come to avenge our broken selves and fight for what's right. God, our father, has ignored us for long enough and yet he still gets to live peacefully. Come now and defend our freedom against those that still believe in him. This is gospel for all fallen angels, angels and archangels alike. Arise, we take the battle now to the most precious place he keeps close to his heart, Earth and the humans.

Those who fight against us, let us revel in their traitorous blood and make it a spectacle to show everyone up in Heaven, on Earth and down in Hell how much God doesn't care, how he's given up, how he doesn't exist anymore."

It's magical to watch. Lucy cares so much and the emotion she puts into the speech comes from the deepest part of her. She believes everything she says.

It's joyous when they come.

Standing amongst thousands of angels and broken souls it occurs to me that we have a chance in making an actual change. I hope Michael doesn't get caught in the crossfire, however much I love him and his unforgivable ways.

Bring on Civil War; I'm waiting for you, and excited to see you. Let's make Earth a battlefield. We wait in silence until they arrive charging closer and closer. The Devil won't be defeated

and neither will I, the imminent storm cursed me my entire life
and I'm not afraid anymore.

I welcome it.

Fragments
by P.T. Holmes

The eighteenth century plantation house loomed in the distance. The 'Axe House' as it was known locally had surrendered to age and decay. The front windows broken. Plants had claimed the house and debris littered the front porch. At the back, ivy had weaved its way up a trellis mounted to the house and a top floor balcony hung besieged by large vines.

Internally, the house fared no better. Termites and wood worm were rampant; half the empire staircase leading to the top floors suffered the most. Dust blanketed every surface and spiders clung to silken webs in the corners of every room. There were mice droppings on the dado rails. Large rodents nested in hidden cupboards and between the paint chipped walls.

The summer heat expansion and winter contraction had caused tiny cracks within the foundations; leaving a brown congealed stain of damp around sheets of peeling floral wallpaper. The Fort Smith 'Axe House' was more than condemned, it was inhospitable.

Lyla knew this. She knew from the moment she found her way inside. She'd rather live here than near her estranged sister. Lyla did not hate Annabelle, contrary to what Annabelle might say or think. What she hated was the awkward conversation, the way Annabelle side-stepped the past. Lyla couldn't escape the past, every time she strapped on her prosthetic arm; it was a constant reminder. She had bigger reasons for returning to this dust bowl town.

After a week inside, the house breathed a life all its own; as if her presence had disturbed the foundations. Most things were easily ignored; sounds of nocturnal vertebrates, a spider clambering over her sleeping bag and a racoon scurrying past her while eating dinner; a cold can of beans. None of these things seemed to bother her. They were justified and explainable, logical even, but other things weren't so easily explained.

The sounds of running through the rooms, bare feet on wood; always too close for comfort but distant and muffled; as if she were listening to the echoes of something that once was there. The echoes of her past. She could hear sounds of talking or whispering, her ears always trying to hone in on the conversation but never quite grasping solid words.

If the strange occurrences weren't enough the house stirred up painful memories for her; it wasn't nicked named the 'Axe House' for nothing.

Lyla refused go near her old blood-stained room; the room where her father read her bedtime stories, the room where he cradled her to sleep and where her brother Blake took an axe to him; injuring her in the process.

Determined not to let the house crawl any further under her skin, Lyla tried to focus on her case files, poring herself over them every night.

The bones of a young boy, found bordering the Arizona border had reopened up the twenty-three year old dormant case, dubbed the 'The Lost Boy' murders. The case involved four victims between six and eight. They were found near Dallas, Albuquerque and Van Buren in early nineties. Most in shallow graves near rivers or in isolated woods. The last remains made the count five.

Speculation spread that the killer – now forgotten –was long dead or incarcerated. When the case crossed Lyla's path, she felt a painful nostalgia hit her hard. Nobody wanted to touch this cold case, not even Lyla but Olivia. Olivia begged Lyla to confront her demons, the nightmares were too much for them both.

Reluctantly, she followed a lead, Timothy Oakland. Timothy had disappeared twenty-three years ago, he was last seen playing with his friend in his front yard, wearing red t-shirt, spider-man shorts and carrying a plastic t-rex. Timothy lived in her childhood town. That's why she'd returned.

Lyla laid the photos out onto the table. Timothy's smiling face on his mother's lap. His mother believed him a victim, not a runaway. She appeared on numerous talk shows and news broadcasts, hoping and praying for information on her missing son. She died five years later, none the wiser of her son's whereabouts.

Lyla watched the old broadcasts on YouTube, hoping for something new. The county police couldn't shed any more light on the case, most of the files were missing or misplaced and every detective that worked the case in the early nineties was now retired or dead.

Lyla spent her days making phone calls, talking to witnesses and family members – those still around. Most of which were dead ends. When she couldn't handle the visceral images anymore or talking to anyone related to the victims, she would find herself wandering the house in the stifling afternoons. Always avoiding that room.

More than once, she stepped into her mother's room, the light pink floral pattern now faded and stained, she could smell her mother's deep spicy perfume and it was if she'd never left. She could see herself lying on her mother's bed in the morning; giggling while watching cartoons. Her mother blowing drying her hair and powdering her face. The same routine she did every weekday for work. A small metal fan blew wafts of patchouli towards her.

Lyla sat on the end of the spring bed, the dresser and thick framed mirror was all that remained.

After moments like this, she longed for LA and her girlfriend Olivia.

Lyla began to find her nights were disturbed by more than just memories, she was dreaming about the victims, the boys from her case files. Their black limbs and bulbous purple bodies and white eyes staring at her, their mouths on the cusp of telling her something—words replaced by black bile trickling from their lips.

She'd wake, a mess of sweat and fear, her red curly hair matted to her face and the stump of her left arm aching with pain. Maybe this case was too close to home? When the nightmares started she contemplated calling Annabelle, but brushed it off.

One night, while skim reading her notes and statements, her face illuminated by tablet screen. She slid her finger across, landing on a photo; a six year old boy lying face down in a shallow grave, deep cuts and bruises littering his back. She scribbled down more notes.

Location: I*solated, privacy*
Motive: S*exual? Possibly sociopath?*
Question: H*ow did he lure the children?*
MO: *Strangulation (under a minute), knife wounds, stabbing, overkill?*

A loud bang sounded on the second floor. Lyla turned her tablet towards the door. In the dim light, she could see someone standing outside. The shadow of their feet peeking underneath. She got up quickly and grasped the handle. As she did so, she heard the faint sound of footsteps moving away.

She swung the door open. Greeted only by dusty air, she rushed towards the stairs.

By the time she reached the ground floor everything was silent. She listened closely, her breathing laboured. She heard nothing but the house creaking its bony structure.

'Jeez Lyla get a grip, you're starting to go nuts.'

Annabelle walked out the maximum security prison, her eyes bloodshot and weary. Inside her car, she struggled to start the engine, the grumble echoing her own frustration. She slumped her head on the wheel for a moment tears threatening to spill. Breathing slowly. Annabelle lifted her head and screamed. Punching the dashboard. Her body thrashing in her seat. Turning the key, the car roared once more before dying.

"YOU FUCK!" she screamed. "You fucking! Fucking FUCK!" She thrashed in her seat, obscenities bursting from her. A man appeared by her window. An elderly man with white hair and grey beard, the collar of his sweat stained shirt undone.

Annabelle jerked when she caught him in her peripheral vision. She closed her eyes, composing herself.

"Sorry Mrs Rayburn, do mind if I talk to you?" he said, leaning his head through the gap in the window.

"Mr Tucker, you startled me. Can I help?" Annabelle said, wiping her face.

"It's regarding your brother ma'am? I know this is not a good time, but as his lawyer I have to follow my client's instructions."

"Instructions? I thought the state was talking care of the funeral arrangements. Surely this isn't regarding a Will, Mr Tucker, you and I both know Blake had nothing of value. Shit everything he owned is in a box— in my trunk."

Annabelle tried her car again, much to her relief the engine sprang to life. She sighed deeply. Mr Tucker looked disheartened; he straightened his tie and placed his hand on the hood of the car.

"Annabelle I am an old man and I've seen many men go to their deaths unfilled. Blake asked me to give you this letter straight after his execution." Mr Tucker pulled out the envelope from his back pocket. "I begrudge doing it now but I am a man of my word. I know what your brother did to you and your sister was… inexcusable. I never knew anyone like him in all my years."

Annabelle turned off her engine and looked directly at the old man. "Mr Tucker, what did my brother want you to tell me?"

"You and your sister," he said, dangling the letter through the window.

"My sister and I are not on the best of terms, I have not spoken to her in years."

"I contacted her firm in LA, they said she's in town, I assumed she would be here… but I suppose, in any case, you should try and contact her, I trust you'll see she reads this letter too?"

Annabelle was surprised to hear her sister was in town, she snatched the letter from Mr Tucker. "I cannot promise anything Mr Tucker but thank you for what you did for Blake, you were like a father to him."

"That's very kind of you, please take care Mrs Rayburn." Annabelle watched as Mr Tucker slipped into his tan sedan.

She looked at the letter, turning it over again and again. Old memories circling her, memories about Blake, about that infamous night, the screaming and the blood.

She turned the key again and the engine sprang to life.

Lyla tossed and turned. The sticky heat clung to her skin. Her dreams were chaotic, flashes of her case juxtaposed with her past. One minute she was five, playing with her brother and sister, laughing hysterically, next she was lying in bed as her father leaned over her and her brother with an axe; a monster behind him.

Then blood and blinding pain. But the pain subsided somehow and she found herself in a stranger's car. She was still a child. She had an arm again. The sensation felt like swimming in thick air.

Blake was sat next to her smiling. "Here, have some more sweets." Lyla watched her hand lift a gummy worm from the bag. She looked down at her legs; she was wearing Spider-Man shorts. Her hair was short and her front teeth were gone.

"Will my mama be there?" she spoke, her voice unfamiliar. She chewed on the gummy.

Then she was walking, following Blake, the location was vaguely familiar. She felt fear and confusion.

"Come on it's not far," the strange voice said from behind her.

Her fear intensified when she realised someone else was near. Within minutes, she was on the ground, fighting to escape the stranger's grip.

Lyla screamed herself awake. Her arm burned, she rubbed it furiously and tried to make sense of her nightmare. Daylight streamed through a small crack in the window.

The front door slammed shut.

Annabelle stepped inside the house, throwing her bag in the corner, half-opened, the contents spilling out. In amongst her belongings was the letter. She bent down to pick up the items. Her eyes pausing on the envelope.

"What the hell are you doing here?" Lyla said, as she crept downstairs.

Annabelle shot up, shoving the letter back into the depths of her bag. Her eyes scanning over Lyla, her hair knotted around her face, her white tank discoloured and her eyes blood shot.

"Lyla! You scared me! What are you doing here?"

"Mind your own business." Lyla brushed past her sister and headed towards the kitchen. She slouched into a rusty chair. Annabelle followed.

"Well?"

"What do you want Annabelle?" Lyla looked at her sister, she was older by five years and Blake was the oldest. Lyla hadn't seen Annabelle since she was in her teens, she hadn't changed much, still dressed like a southern belle from a bygone era with one altercation, her red hair now dyed blonde. Annabelle looked just like their mother. Lyla felt a surge of discomfort in her gut.

Annabelle sat down opposite, her chair wobbled as she did. She dabbed at the perspiration on her face.

"I see you've made yourself right at home here," she said, looking around the kitchen, a large generator stood half in and out of the pantry in the far corner, and a coffee pot sat on the counter nearby. The sink was riddle with dishes; cockroaches scurried over them.

"Let's not play niceties. I have a headache and I am tired."

"Okay, first off you look like shit and you still haven't answered my question?"

"I am working a case in town. Figured I'd save some money. What brings you home sweet home?"

"I don't know, guess after today I felt it necessary to pay my respects—"

"Respects?" Lyla looked at her sister confused unsure of what she really meant. Annabelle shuffled in her chair.

"You don't know what today is do you?"

"Should I?"

Annabelle felt a pang of betrayal, she hated how things ended up so bitter between them. "Blake's execution," she said, choking back her tears. What hurt the most was Lyla's ignorance towards him.

Lyla looked up, her chest tightened, she could not be sure if it was from relief or grief.

"That was today?"

"This morning. Blake's lawyer's been trying to contact you. He told me you were in town but I never thought I'd find you here." Annabelle collected herself.

"Why are you so upset?" Lyla stood up and started pacing. "Maybe we should celebrate, isn't that what you're supposed to do after these occasions?"

"Don't be so crude Lyla. He was our brother!"

"Are you going to tell me that there is more to this than meets the eye? That I should understand how troubled my brother was, that I was too young to understand? Fuck you Annabelle!" Lyla was shaking with anger.

They sat in silence, Annabelle gave up trying to speak; as she stood up ready to leave, a loud thud sounded from upstairs. Both girls looked up at the ceiling.

"Are you alone?"

"Yes, there is no one else here—" Lyla paused, remembering. "Actually I haven't been in, my old room."

"You've been here all this time and you haven't checked your room, at all?"

Lyla shook her head.

Annabelle rushed towards her bag, rummaging for a moment, she pulled out a small white handled gun.

"What are doing Anna?" Lyla went after her sister towards the door. Lyla snatched the gun from her.

"What the hell! I can handle myself you know!"

"So can I." Lyla pushed past her sister. Annabelle followed her upstairs.

The girls stood by the doorway of Lyla's childhood. The door closed, Lyla held the gun in her right hand, she moved her leg and positioned it against the frame. "On three," she said.

Annabelle nodded from behind her sister, her heart racing.

"One! Two! Three!" Lyla pushed the door open, poised and ready to shoot.

What greeted them was nothing but stale air and streams of motes floating in the hazy afternoon sun.

"See? it was probably an animal," Lyla said, putting her hand down. She moved behind Annabelle.

"What's this doing here?" Annabelle said bending down, lifting up a faded plastic t-rex from the middle of the bloodstained wooden floor.

Lyla was already making her way downstairs, ignoring her sister and more than eager to get away from that room. Half-way down, a loud crash sounded in the kitchen. Lyla ran as fast as she could, the gun still in hand.

"Ok buddy, unless you'd like an ass full of bullets, I'd quit playing games!" Lyla pointed the gun into the room.

There was nothing but a smashed coffee pot lying on floor.

Lyla exhaled slamming the gun down onto the vinyl table.

"What the hell happened here?" Annabelle's words made Lyla jump.

"Nothing, probably a rodent or something." Lyla sat down again, her head felt heavy and thick.

"I found this, you left before I could show you." Annabelle handed Lyla the toy.

"You kidding me right?" Lyla said examining the t-rex, bits of the painted face peeling on to her fingers.

"I swear I found it in your old room!"

"This has to be a prank?" Lyla put the t-rex onto the kitchen table.

"Who is pranking us, who knows you're here?"

"Nobody, only Olivia."

"Olivia? Oh, Right your girlfriend."

Lyla shot Annabelle a look.

"Relax, I am open minded."

"Yeah, right,"

"Lyla, could you at least try and talk to me…"

Lyla reached over the table and slid her tablet towards Annabelle. She clicked the screen open. The corpse of a boy appeared. His bleached white skin protruding from green shrubbery. His hands and bulbous torso extended and purple.

Annabelle's expression changed. Her face turned ashen and she pushed the tablet away. She leaned herself back against the sink.

"That's why I am here, happy?"

Annabelle wanted to give Lyla the letter and leave. She regretted returning to the house. The heinous image reminded her of the scared injured little Lyla from their past. She could hear six-year old Lyla screaming for her mother. As much as she wanted to leave, she knew she had to fulfil Blake's wishes.

"I think its best I spend the night, just to make sure no one is squatting here."

Lyla did not respond as her sister left. She knelt on floor collecting pieces of glass, her own tears diluting the coffee on the floor.

Annabelle returned to the house, Lyla was napping next to her files. Annabelle placed two large paper bags on the counter, inadvertently waking up her sister.

"Anything else happen while I was gone?"

Lyla ignored her. Annabelle rolled her eyes and began to unpack the shopping. A new coffee pot, ready meals and a bag of gummy candy.

"Why did you buy this? Lyla said lifting up the paper bag of confectionary, a strange sensation of deja-vu came over her. Flashes of her nightmare sprang to mind.

"I don't know, a treat?" Annabelle shrugged oblivious to Lyla's discomfort.

Lyla threw the bag into a rusted tin garbage can.

"What did you do that for?" Annebelle said. "That's it! What is going on with you?"

Lyla didn't have the strength to talk, she walked past her sister, tablet in hand and up to her temporary room; folding herself into her sleeping bag.

Lyla tried to nap. In her dark and damp room she felt tugging at her bag. She moved her feet, her head pounding. In between consciousness she felt the tugging again, "Annabelle?"

Lyla turned towards the door, in the darkness she could make out a form.

"Seriously can we not do this right now."

The more she stared at the figure, the darker it looked. Lyla turned over, a small rodent scurried past her face and she jolted up wiping her face and patting down her bag. "Damn rats!"

She leaned over and lifted her tablet. She searched her notes, wrestling with her headache and exhaustion. Her eyes closing for second.

A cool breeze roused her. She looked towards the door way, the shadowy figure was gone. The tablet wasn't in her hands. She searched for it. "What the hell?" she muttered as she groped around her sleeping bag and the floor. "Annabelle are you messing with me?"

A light flashed in the middle of the room. Lyla's eyes followed the source. There in the dark hanging mid-air was her tablet.

Lyla shook her head and wiped her face. The tablet remained suspended, as her eyes adjusted. Someone was holding it. The shape of person, the shape of child. Lyla gasped.

The tugging started again and she instantly looked down at her feet.

Two tiny black hands gripped hold of her sleeping bag. She sat frozen as she watched the hands move closer, a black decaying figure writhing and slithering into focus as it moved its way onto her legs.

Annabelle walked to her car to collect the extra bits she'd bought. Dusk had turned from light evening hues to dark blue. Annabelle lifted the paper bag and turned to face the house, the air around her changed and a cold chill crept past her, drawing her eyes to the house. She searched each window and froze. There on the third floor, the last corner window, a figure stood staring straight at her.

Dropping the bags, Annabelle ran into the house, fearing the worst. She peaked through the door to check on Lyla. She could make out the vague shape of her sister under her sleeping bag, Annabelle continued to the third floor.

Lyla's childhood bedroom door was open. Annabelle was certain she had closed it when she found the toy. Swallowing her fear, she entered.

There standing by the window was Lyla, her eyes glazed and blank, she didn't speak or turn towards Annabelle.

"Lyla, what the fuck are you doing here... Lyla speak to me! I just saw you in bed! How did you get here?" A chill ran up Annabelle's spine. Annabelle grabbed Lyla, shaking her. Lyla didn't respond.

She walked a mute and expressionless Lyla to her room. There on the floor was Lyla's tablet and the toy. The screen lit up. Words flashed by...

'Mommy! Bad Man! Help.... HELP HELP! I wan go home now...'

The screen went blank. Lyla looked at Annabelle, "Did you see that?" she said, dazed and confused.

Annabelle sighed. "Now you talk! let's just get downstairs."

Lyla couldn't rest, and Annabelle watched helplessly as her sister tossed and turned. Her sleepy words echoing her nightmares. "How can I help you? How..."

Annabelle silently, her mind focused on Lyla when a she heard a sound in the kitchen. Reluctantly, Annabelle stood up, listening carefully, she could make out faint sounds of foots steps. She entered the kitchen, there on the table was Blake's envelope. Annabelle felt a familiar chill and looked for her bag; it was still by the front door.

Impossible!

Lyla trudged her way to the kitchen; the smell of coffee permeating through the damp and mould.

"Morning," Lyla looked at her sister in surprise. "You're still here?"

"I don't scare easily. What happened with you last night?"

"I don't know." Lyla poured herself a coffee.

Annabelle looked away, her eyes filled with tears; she slid a creased envelope across the table. "Did you take this from my bag?"

Lyla looked at her sister confused. "What are you talking about?"

"Just tell me the truth, did you take the envelope from my bag?"

Lyla sat down, she picked up the letter turning it over. "Why would I take this from you?"

"Then why was it on the kitchen table, it was in my bag."

"Maybe it's the ghost?" Lyla said.

"Are you serious? Don't be so ridiculous, that fucking case is going straight to your head!"

Lyla leaned back in her chair; despite last night's encounter she wasn't afraid. The encounter had given her clarity. Annabelle had witnessed the strange occurrences too.

"I'm not crazy, I can't explain it but I think they're talking to me."

"Who?"

"The victims... I've been having dreams but they don't make any sense. Blake's there and someone else, I'm me but not... last night! You saw, you saw the tablet and you found the t-rex—the t-rex, where is it?" Lyla searched the kitchen.

"It's in your room. I don't understand what you're talking about?" Annabelle moved closer to Lyla. "Maybe you need to get more sleep? Just let this go for one night."

"I can't let this go. Why here? Why now? Why me?"

"Lyla can you hear yourself right now! There are no such things as ghosts, get a grip!"

Lyla ignored her sister and ran upstairs, there on the floor lay the t-rex.

Back in the kitchen, Lyla ripped open her files, pulling them apart, searching for a photo.

"Look Anna, look!"

Annabelle stood staring at her sister, clutching a small polaroid photo. She took the photo from her sister; in it was

Timothy Oakland smiling on his mother's lap, holding the t-rex toy.

"It's the same toy! This is not coincidence!"

"Lyla please, these toys were common back then, maybe Blake had one? You're freaking me out. We need to talk."

"Talk about what?" Lyla sat down.

Annabelle inhaled deeply. "Blake had his reasons for what happened... there's a reason why—"

"I don't want to hear why... you always take his side!"

"Sides, nobody is taking sides, for goodness sake Lyla will listen! You need read this! Just know that we knew no other way to stop him."

"We? Now you're sounding crazy."

"Read the letter if you want to know the truth." Annabelle grabbed her bag and headed towards the front door.

"Why are you leaving?"

"I can't..."

Lyla watched as her car sped out of the gravel drive way.

She opened the letter, her brother's scrawled writing greeted her.

Dear Annabelle and Lyla,

I never intended to write this letter, I had hoped I would never need to write this. I cannot justify my actions but you must know I did not mean to harm you, Lyla. That night, I intended only to hurt him. To stop the suffering. I never wanted to hurt you. Annabelle and I agreed that we would never reveal what happened. I promised myself I would die with the truth. I can never ask you to forgive me. I did what he wanted, he killed them. I didn't want to kill anyone. They trusted me and I betrayed them. I watched them die. I was so afraid I couldn't save them. Dad was the devil.

"You are of your father the devil, and you want to do the desires of your father, He was a murderer from the beginning,

37

and does not stand in the truth because there is no truth in him, Whenever he speaks a lie, he speaks from his own nature, for he is a liar and the father of lies."

I am paying for my sins, I ask no one but my Heavenly Father for forgiveness. I pray that those boys have found peace. I pray for you both. Find each other. Forgive each other. My only request is that you destroy that home.

Burn it to the ground!

- Blake Adams.

Lyla paced the house. Her head throbbed again, her eyes burned from endless salty tears and her mouth ached from shouting and cursing. She kicked at the walls. Exhausted, she fell on the floor, her body twisted in the foetal position. By the time she woke up, her body shivered, the house now colder. A cold that lingers in bones of your fingers and toes.

Rubbing the sleep from her face, her muscles felt weighted and heavy. Lyla manoeuvred herself to the kitchen, her eyes trying to adjust to the darkness. The coffee had gone cold, but she poured herself a cup anyway and sat down. Her tablet sat on the surface; she had no memory of bringing it downstairs. She took a sip of coffee and then spat the vile, vinegary liquid straight back out.

Her tablet switched on, images of each boy's remains flashed, faster and faster before stopping on missing picture of Timothy. Lyla studied the image, remembering last night.

Oh my god.

The evidence came together in her mind.

A small hand appeared above her tablet, the light hitting the underside. A boy's hand, decayed and one of its finger's missing. Lyla screamed and flung herself from the chair towards the backdoor.

"Timothy?" she whispered. Towards the basement, she heard the faint echoes giggling and running. She followed the sound. There in the darkness on the concrete basement floor was the toy and Blake's letter.

She stared at it when Timothy appeared; a fully formed boy; he was skeletal and pale with protruding purple veins. His torso full red raw injuries and his mouth black. He pointed at the floor.

Annabelle did not go home. Instead, she drove for over an hour before returning to the house. There was an ominous feeling. The lights were off. Annabelle wondered how her sister took the letter. *Has she put the pieces together?*

Annabelle knew only fragments of her brother's and father's involvement in the 'Lost Boy Murders'.

As child she had watched her father manipulate everyone, he had an unnatural charisma and charm. One night in the abandoned barn bordering their family plantation, a ten year old Annabelle found her fourteen year old brother attempting to take his life. When she confronted him, he confessed to his and their fathers part in the murders.

Together they hatched a plan to kill him. The plan succeeded and failed. Lyla got hurt, their mother was institutionalised, their family ripped apart and irrevocably broken.

She entered the house; in her mind she swore this would be the last time.

"Lyla?" She called. She heard banging from the kitchen. *Not again,* she thought. The house was shrouded in black, the moon illuminated parts of Lyla, who was dragging in large tools from the yard outside and throwing them down into the basement.

"What are you doing?" Lyla seemed possessed, she did not acknowledge Annabelle. Lyla dragged the sledgehammer and with all her strength threw it down the wooden steps of the basement. The hammer landed with a mighty thud on the stone floor. Lyla wiped her hands on her jeans.

"Lyla? Please talk to me?"

"How long did you know?"

"Long enough, I didn't know much, Blake kept some of the details quiet."

"All these years? All those victims? Their families? Not once did you or Blake fess up?"

"Blake was serving his time for Dad's murder... Everything happened so quickly. Hurting you was never part of the plan."

"I don't know who to hate more, you or Blake... But Dad? All this time... I cried about his death, I blamed myself. I tortured myself over what happened! I was six-years old!"

"You don't think I didn't? I wanted to tell you for so long but I just couldn't bring myself to have that stigma on our family, you still had a chance at a normal life..."

"There is nothing normal about any of this." Lyla turned from Annabelle and headed into the blackness of the basement.

Reluctantly, Annabelle followed.

"I have to know, he's here and I have to set him free." Lyla looked at her sister, her eyes red rimmed and her hair tightly tied. She pulled out a flashlight from her back pocket.

"This is crazy! You're going to dig up the basement?"

Lyla rolled the torch towards Annabelle, "I want the truth and I'll do whatever I can to get it. Either help me or get out."

Annabelle picked up the torch and a stream of yellow light lit the concrete floor.

Lyla lifted a sledgehammer, she pounded on the concrete; each consecutive blow made the house flinch. Particles of sand coated her brow. She continued hit the floor, pausing only to wipe her face.

After thirty minutes of pounding, Lyla reached soil. She threw the sledgehammer and grabbed the shovel near Annabelle, who watched in silence.

The body wasn't far from the surface, less than two feet. Annabelle gasped in horror nearly dropping the torch.

Wrapped in a plastic sheet were Timothy Oakland's remains. His Spider-Man clothes scattered near him. The dry soil had leathered his skin, his cherub baby face replaced by a shrunken skull. His left hand missing a finger.

"Oh my god!" Annabelle said.

Lyla knelt next to the body. She reached down to the strawberry-blonde tuft of hair on his head, she touched it tentatively. "I found you." Lyla lifted her head towards her sister. Annabelle moved closer; Lyla seemed so small and vulnerable. Annabelle paused momentarily before touching her sister.

"I am so sorry."

The sisters held each other for a while, crying and trying to decide how best to handle Timothy. They carried his remains outside. It didn't take long for Annabelle to dig another hole; they buried him and placed the toy as marker on his grave.

They sat in the kitchen one last time. Lyla covered in sweat sand and soil, her red hair looked grey under the light of the moon.

"What now?"

"I don't know. No one's going to believe us. It's not like we can bring him to justice now."

"Do think there are more buried down there?" Annabelle said tapping on the kitchen table, her dirt covered hands shaking.

"No but Dad travelled a lot, so maybe there are more out there. I want to find them."

"Why?"

"They deserve to be set free, that's what Timothy wanted. Blake did too."

"You still think it was a ghost luring you to his grave?"

"Maybe, I don't know. I don't think I am psychic." Lyla lifted Blake's letter from the table. She read it again.

"Did he suffer?"

"All his life... It was quick... I suppose he found peace."

"I'm not ready for all the details but maybe one day we can talk about it?"

"I'd like that." Annabelle reached for Lyla's hand and held it.

The house looked like a shell. It sighed with relief as Lyla poured the gasoline onto the floors and splashed it across the walls. Lyla passed the kitchen table, dousing the letter.

The sisters walked together, a trail of gasoline following them out of the front door. Annabelle took the match box; she flicked it across and dropped it in the puddle before them. The flames leaped up and spidered their way back along the path, engulfing the porch and screen door.

Within minutes the whole house was ablaze, the flames licking at the walls and every surface it could find. Blackening the peeling wallpaper, covering the congealed stains and bathing the stairs in fire.

Lyla looked into the distance, her eyes focusing on the smoke. There stood Timothy smiling, he looked just like his photo, he waved his hand at Lyla, next to him was a woman; his mother. As the smoke thickened and blew across them, obscuring them from view; they disappeared.

Neither of sisters spoke. They just watched the house burn.

The Undertaker
by Samuel Long

The machine lets out a cold, sharp shrill

"You have three new messages. Message one:"

"Hi, James," a women's voice called. "This is Dr Sutton from the—"

"Message deleted. Message two:"

"Hello. My name is Mellissa Morris," the voice began... *Probably another client,* he thought as he sipped through his morning coffee. "I have called to request your services as a funeral director," the woman's voice trembled a little, "My father has recently passed away… He was a good man."

The name Morris did have a ring of familiarity to it. He weighed it in his mind as the message continued.

"His name was Jonathan Morris. Have you heard of him? I remember him mentioning he was acquainted with your father. You probably don't remember him though. It was a long time ago."

James' heart quickened, blow upon blow was dealt to his ribcage as he struggled to utter anything other than stifle a short gasp.

"That doesn't really matter now though," the woman continued. "Please get back to me so I can start making preparations. Thank you." The line clicked.

"End of message. Message three..."

He remembered now, John Morris. He had indeed been a good friend to his father. In a time of desperation, he had turned to John years ago when business was slow and money was short. Now business had picked up again and he'd knew he would have had to have paid back his debts.

"'ello, Mr Syler," the caller spoke roughly, as though it were choking, coughing and sputtered between each word, and he could hear the wet, smacking sound of the man's lips as they opened and closed with each uttering.

"I's just callin'… to let ye know, that, that, the job is done."

"What job?" he found himself speaking aloud.

"The…job…to take 'are—" the man was breathing heavily. Gasping. He coughed and spluttered and wetted his lips again before speaking. "To take 'are of your debt."

He froze at the sudden coincidence of the call and John Morris' death. He looked down to find the cup in his hand was shaking; droplets of black coffee drained into a dark blotch that spread deep into the fabric of the floor, like a visible corruption that could not be removed.

He didn't have any debt. Not now anyway.

What could it mean? Were they connected?

"I took 'are of it. Expect my payment soon."

"End of messages."

Those words startled him. He had heard them before. *Expect my payment soon.* The phrase rattled inside his head, ungraspable, mocking him as he tried to dig up the memory. Images. Patchy and disjointed. He had been drunk. He rarely drank. The throbbing in his head told him that much. Johnathan Morris had met him in a bar, told him those exact words. *"I'll expect my payment soon,"* he would say, between each deep swallow of foaming beer, greedily taking on more than he needed. *Greedy.* He gulped down another mouthful of beer. Drinking, drinking, drinking, but never quite satisfied.

The next image was a blur. James had money sure but not the kind that John Morris thought he did. James drank to rival his opponent. He drank and smiled. He had stumbled into the bathroom, angry, alone and drunk. He wallowed in piss and fear. He had to come up with the money. He had been an undertaker all his life. His father trained him and his grandfather trained his father. Without that, where was he? He remembered the light, how it flickered in the restroom On and off, light and dark, an epilepsy of uncertainty; uncertain thoughts, uncertain answers. Unanswerable questions. Then it came to him.

How can I make this problem go away?

One of the lightbulbs above him exploded, casting a bottomless shadow that he felt himself fall into. Sparks of dying light fell on him, burning the fabric of his suit. Amidst the dim light of the other bulbs, he saw the man standing there, watching; their eyes mirroring each other. He was tall, bald and overpowering, thick wide shoulders and great pulsing arms. He spoke with a crooked smile on his face. James told the man his situation, felt he could confide in him. The man just nodded, that crooked smile unwavering.

"What would you have me do?" his crooked mouth voiced.

The pieces began to fall into place; like a well-crafted puzzle, a picture was formed.

"It's the only way…"

The man's smile grew even wider. That crooked smile.

The bell that hung above the door danced at the entrance of a new customer, beckoning James Syler's attention.

It was late in the afternoon now and he had disregarded all notions of his involvement with John Morris' death, chalking it up to mere coincidence and an overanxious mind. The newspaper that lay spread on his desk had made mention of the death, how police were *"looking in to all possible leads."* His eyes glanced away from the paper to the figure walking through the door.

The first thing that drew his attention was her sculpted beauty; high, chilled cheekbones, vibrant skin, lakes of shimmering blue that seemed to have awoken from her idol like face. Her nose was puffy and red from the cold or from crying and yet it only added to her charm.

"Hello, miss. How can I help?"

"Are you James Syler?" she sniffed.

"I am," he said with a smile.

"I left a message for you, about requiring your services?"

"Ah yes. I'm terribly sorry for not getting back to you on that, it's been rather a busy day. You must be Mellissa Morris?"

She said nothing, only her cold and distant eyes flickered for a moment in acknowledgement.

45

"I'm sorry for your loss. I understand that this will be a troubling time for you and your family and I will do everything I can do to make this process as easy for you as possible."

Ignoring the fact, I may have been involved in his death— No, no, no, that was just a coincidence.

"Would you like to come into the lounge and we can make the appropriate arrangements?"

Stop thinking about it James. You're here to do business.

She nodded and moved towards the back room. James followed behind her. On his way through the doorway, he spied the flashing red light of the answering machine, blinking furiously. The coffee stain had rooted itself in the crème rug. He had cleaned it up as best as he could but, but for some reason, in the dull lighting of the room, the stain seemed to have grown.

The lounge was underwhelming to say the least. It consisted of two chairs that stood opposite each other, with a stumpy coffee table in between. Pressed against the wall was a faded, patchy sofa.

"I assume you have the death certificate with you?" James began once they had both sat down. He could tell by the sudden but brief expression on her face that she was already uncomfortable.

"I do." She lifted it from her back, glanced at it for a moment as though to conform the name John Morris was there. Her delicate, long fingers trembled as she passed it to him.

"Let's see here." James continued, murmuring various details as his eyes inspected each and every box. *Name: John Morris. Sex: Male. Date of Birth: 3/7/1964. Date of Death: 28/11/15. Cause of Death—*

"Strangulation?" he started.

"Yes." She sighed, closing her eyes as though she were blind to the sadness of the world.

"I am terribly sorry," he consoled her.

"It's fine." She sniffed again.

Then it was true, he thought. *John Morris had indeed been murdered.*

The affair took up most of the afternoon and when Mellissa Morris left, the sky had been covered in a black curtain. James made the various arrangements for the funeral of Mellissa's father. The day had been long and he was tired. Doors were locked and shutters pulled down. Contented, he headed down the hallway, towards his house at the back. The stain on the floor remained unchanged. The light on the machine kept blinking red, casting a crimson glow as he watched it work. On and off and on and off. His finger hesitated over the button.

What am I so worried about? I had nothing to do with John Morris's death. It wasn't my fault he was so greedy and it definitely wasn't me who killed him. It was the man I met from before.

His finger lingered once more. *Best leave it for tomorrow.* He wandered back into the house.

He had taken no more than three steps when the phone rang. He drowned in the noise of its drone; the phone caught its breath, stopped, then started all over again. He was compelled to answer. Taking three steps back, he lifted the receiver.

"Hello?" said James.

"'ello Mr Syler." The croaking splutter of the other line began.

"Who is this?"

"You know who this is."

"Why the hell are you calling me?"

"You believe you are not to blame for the death of John Morris, that you should be… absolved."

"I had nothing to do with that. You were the one who killed him!"

The man laughed cruelly. "We both know you had much a 'and in this as I did."

"How dare you expect me to take the blame on this. I did nothing wrong!"

"You 'ere the one that pointed me to him. Your 'and's are just as bloody as mine."

"Don't get me involved in what you did!"

"Mr Syler, you sound angry? I only helped you in your time of desperate need. You should be thanking me."

"Thanking you? I never expected you to bloody do it!"

"Ah but I did and now you and I are in the same boat. When I go down, you'll go down."

"Is that a threat?" James felt his legs shake, whether from anger or fear he couldn't quite tell.

"No," the voice coughed. "But it is a fact."

James felt something cold gripping in his chest; something clamped around his heart, squeezing until it would burst. He toppled over in pain as though out of nowhere, he had been dealt a punch to the gut. His face fell to the dark stain of coffee on the rug at his feet, as tall and wide as his shadow. He took large, deep breaths, each time inhaling faster until he uttered a wheezing cough.

"Are you okay, Mr Syler?"

There had to be a way out of this. He couldn't go down for a crime that he didn't commit. There had to be an escape. *How do I make this problem go away?*

"I'll pay you," James said.

"'cuse me?" The man horsed.

"I will pay you."

"For what?"

"I will pay for your silence."

"No you won't."

"Yes I will. We can work something out. We can pretend like this never happened."

"Oh but it has happened, Mr Syler, ain't no escaping that."

"We can both walk away from this. What do you say?"

"You're trying to make a deal? Get me to walk away so that you won't be implicated in my crimes?"

"I'll pay you though."

There was a brief second of silence as though the world and all who inhabited it held their breath with anticipation.

"I'm afraid I can't do that." The line clicked.

"What do you mean… Hello? Hello?! You fucking bastard get back here! Don't you dare leave me like this! We had a deal!"

The early dawn sun broke over the horizon. Strands of light slipped through the glass windows of the undertaker's store, yet despite this, James Syler sat in darkness. He lay crumpled beside the blinking red light of the machine, wrapped in the fibres of the rug, not sure where the rug ended and the stain began.

What now? he thought to himself. *Where do I go from here?*

The voice of the morning news echoed from the lounge.

"…Police have disclosed that a witness to the John Morris murder has been found and brought in for questioning…"

"Only a matter of time now," he muttered.

James Syler had thought we was a good man. He had been raised on the morals of his mother and his only goal was to follow in his father's footsteps, that would have made him proud. He hadn't thought or wanted anything else in life. Maybe if he had, he wouldn't be here now. Maybe if he had, he wouldn't have tried so desperately to save it. Now everything would be gone and he could do nothing to stop it. He had been living on borrowed time. A long time. Whatever punishment awaited him was patient and methodical. He had thought the police would appear, or his friend on the phone would come with worse news, or to point the finger and cry between his wetted lips and crocked smile: "It was him! He wanted John Morris dead!"

When would it end?

Where would the stain of his corruption end?

Where?

When will the police get here?

When will this torment end?

When would it end?

Soon, he told himself. *Soon.*

The phone left out a vile cry. He jumped out of the darkness of his despair. He let the phone ring and ring and ring…

"'ello…" he spoke. Coughed and spoke again "Hello."

Nothing.

"Listen, if this is you again, I'm going to hang up—"

"HELP ME!" A man's voice shouted. Then came a gasp. It echoed and wheezed and gargled as though something were clawing, digging its way out of his throat. The man seemed desperately short of air and every hazardous cry for help was quieter and more hopeless than the last.

"Why?" the man croaked.

"Because you deserve it," James found himself saying.

There was silence. Coughing. Wheezing. Breathing.

Then finally, a whisper "You killed me, James Syler. Only you."

The line clicked.

James felt something burn in the pit of his stomach. Something rose to his chest, he flexed his hand and the phone was thrown, shattered, and the shrapnel struck him. He screamed in pain and anger, felt hot blood run down his face. He stumbled from his seat and made his way to a mirror. He trailed his way into the bathroom, flicked the switch and light dawned his face, illuminating his cut. His eyes gazed into the mirror, his mirror and saw the dark, cold eyes of a killer. His eyes. He noticed how tall he was, how he towered over everything small and breakable. He wiped the sweat away from his bald head with his course hands, noticing how thick his shoulders were. He was truly unsightly. Maybe that was why he had decided to work among the dead. The dead don't complain, the dead don't make threats. They don't hand out loans. *They simply are.*

"You're not looking good, eh James?" He laughed to himself, wiping away the blood from the cut on his face. He smiled. It was a crooked smile, teeth never quite in the right place. "You 'ere responsible for his death, an' the ones before that an' the ones before that. Ain't no use denying it now." *No use denying it now…*

He reached into the cupboard and retrieved the razor. He placed it under his neck and began to shave, the blade skipping across his skin. He always looked like a new man with a clean cut. Tiny black fragments fell into the sink. He washed himself, baptised himself with a new name. *Hyde.* He liked it. *James Hyde.* He let the name play on his lips for a while, familiarising himself with it, finding the best accent to accompany it. He washed away his sins under that name, changed his clothes into something more basic; jeans and a flannel shirt. He picked up the suitcase that waited for him at the door. He paused for a brief second, thinking that he had forgotten something important. He walked across the hallway, across the crème rug, bent down behind the small stand and unplugged the phone. The red light which had remained awake for the ordeal, recording everything, finally slept.

James Hyde walked out of the door, leaving his old life behind.

Jane's Master Meals
by Rory Kenny

Jane awoke baffled.

After a second, she rolled over to check the clock: 4:47am. She turned back in relief, she had not missed the alarm.

Jane lay still, trying to fall back to sleep. It didn't work. She wriggled in bed trying to force herself into a comfortable position, but nothing helped. It wasn't how she lay that was keeping her awake

She looked over at her husband, Shaun, snoring away. He was a big beefy man who had trouble sleeping, but when he did, he was lost to the world. They had been married for seventeen years and with each one passing, the romance withered away. They had become a couple who lived together annd nothing more. If it weren't for their son she would've left.

Trying to sleep was useless.

She got up and took a long, early shower which was probably the only time she ever usually had to herself, got dressed and headed downstairs where her son, Tim, was already at the table eating his cereal.

Jane prepared herself a ham sandwich, she loved meat and this was fresh from the butchers. As a restaurant chef, the meat had to be fresh.

"Looking forward to school today?" she asked Tim.

"No," he replied aggressively.

"Come now, cheer up for me today? Otherwise we will have to cancel your party on Saturday."

The threat worked. Tim sat up straight and kept quiet while he munched on his cereal. Jane bit into her sandwich and forgot all her troubles.

Seven o'clock came and she hustled Tim into the car as she prepared for the school run. The lunch box was her favourite part; she took pride in that. She knew the other mums supplied an apple, yoghurt and a sandwich which always ended up crumpled in the foil and all of the possible tastes wasted. Tim's lunch box was more flavourful, a wrap with chicken, peaches and a small pouch smoothie.

As she clipped Tim into his seatbelt, Shaun came out, said hello and hurried off. The grandest gesture of love he had given her in a while. *Fat pig,* she thought as he waddled down the driveway. Jane composed herself, got into the car and drove off to school. The car journey was filled with usual chatter about wanting Tim to have a good day.

She arrived to the restaurant and hurried in as she was already late. Thankfully she was head chef and no one was brave enough to berate her for tardiness. She got dressed quickly into her uniform and she felt like a different, stronger woman under the chef's hat, delicate with a knife and cunning under pressure.

As the day went on it was relatively quiet, but Jane was no novice. Come noon it would be packed, the restaurant was the only one close enough to the business area. She knew big and wealthy businessmen loved to dine in extravagance.

The unforgiving lunch time came and something had to go wrong. Marie, a clumsy chef, was holding a pot of boiling water and her grip loosened as she tried to move it. Just slipping through her fingers, the pot crashed, spilling all the water over the floor. Jane stopped what she was cutting and turned to the scene of the crime. The anxious look on Marie's face spoke volumes.

"What were you thinking? Why didn't you ask for help? Are you stupid? It's just common sense for God's sake!"

Marie cowered from Jane trying to apologise, but it was no use.

Jane took herself aside to calm herself down, breathing slowly; *in out... in out.*
In and out.

53

Whilst driving back, Jane was still surprised at how angry she'd been. It slowly consumed her, the poor girl had been trying to do her job. *I'll say sorry to her tomorrow,* she thought. But the temper still bubbled away. In a strange way it felt good to let herself feel.

At home, Shaun lay inside on the couch. She gave an audible groan and continued to the kitchen, her heartbeat ringing in her ears and her hands curled into fists. She couldn't focus on anything other than the pure rage from earlier, the first time she had felt alive in years.

Shaun walked into the kitchen. "When's dinner?" he asked.

"Why don't you make it yourself?" she replied.

"Excuse me?"

She turned around Shaun was starting at her, his expression slack. She could tell he'd been drinking and she knew what would come next. Suddenly the anger vanished.

"I—I I mean it's only early!" she said, trying to justify the response but it didn't matter.

It was too late.

He grabbed her by the throat and pinned her against the counter. She squirmed, but couldn't break his firm grip. Passive eyes stared deep into her, getting under her skin. Panic brought back her rage in a rush. Fighting to breathe, she grobed across the kitchen counter. Her fingers closed around the handle of a knife and before she could think, it went up and down, deep into Shaun's neck.

Time changes. He coughs blood into her face. His eyes widen and his face clouds with baffled hurt. His grip on her loosens and he stumbles back. His hands clutching at the wound in his throat.

Jane fiddles around the fat and fingers on his neck; she places two fingers just under his chin and listens, just listens.

"That must have severed some sort of precious artery."

It had.

Shaun stepped back, his ruby face became pale and like a falling tree he fell hard onto the kitchen floor.

Blood splattered everywhere. *Not on the carpet, not on the carpet* Jane prayed. Shaun shuddered, red foam came from his mouth and trickled down his cheek. Jane got down to her knees and held him tight, finally seeing the young Shaun she'd once loved. She held him and wouldn't let go, trying to ease him through the pain. He tried to shout but could only gurgle through the bubbling blood in his mouth.

He began to spasm and Jane held him tighter, forcing him onto his back on the kitchen tiles.

Finally, with a big jolt, the life left him.

For a long time, Jane sat there with Shaun's head in her hands. She felt calm and distant from everything. She wasn't sure how long she sat before what she'd done sank in.

Shaun's dead. I killed him.

She got to her feet, hurried to the bathroom and threw all her clothes into the tub and turned the tap on. She threw bleach on them, stepped into the shower and scrubbed her body fiercely, her mind flitting from one idea to get rid of the body to another impossible, plan B. She got out the shower and made a decision.

Naked, she went back downstairs, The kitchen knives were all over the table. She picked up the largest and set about Shaun's clothes, cutting them away and making them into a big bloodstained pile. She carried that up to the bath and came back. Her apron was hanging on the door. She put it on. In an instant, she became head chef and Shaun became prime beef or pork from the butcher. Skillfully, she started to chop his body up into smaller pieces, using the knives to carve well-weighed chunks of meat off of the bone. *Human flesh, like pork,* she thought. No longer Shaun just meat, meat she'd worked with for years.

Finally, she was done. All the unusable parts gathered up in six black bin bags, the rest, piled high on the kitchen counter, as if it had come straight from the butcher.

Not bad for an off the cuff job, she thought.

Tim climbed into the car and as soon as he did, Jane felt very empty.

"How was your day at school?" she asked.

As usual he didn't reply, but sat in silence, staring blankly out the window.

The journey was not far, but it seemed to take forever. Her hands were still sticky and stained from moving the bags, but Tim didn't notice. When they arrived home he ran straight upstairs into his room, already trying to lock himself out from the world. Jane followed him up,

"Hey Tim, don't come down for a bit... I've got some work to do, so don't go asking for dinner or anything else."

He grunted. This was clear to Jane he'd acknowledged the request. However, just to be safe, she took the chair on the balcony and propped it against the door before going back downstairs.

She laid out plastic sheets across the dining table, collected her spices and laid them to one side. Jane opened the fridge, tore the bags open and looked down at the chopped pieces of her husband.

Saw nothing but pure meat.

She took out two steaks and placed them on the counter. They were obscenely beautiful.

The professional chef kicked in and she became lost in her work. Oven at a low heat, marinading sauce bubbling away in a pan. She was having a field day, applying all of her special spices and herbs. Making sure everything was seasoned and prepared, it had to be perfect before she put it in the oven. Two done, two more came out of the fridge, then two more and two more and so on, until the fridge was aempty and both trays of the oven were filled.

Jane was going to low cook the meat through the night to make it moist. The masterpiece of her plan was committed, her magnum opus almost. All she had to do now was wait for tomorrow and the evidence would be gone.

It had got dark. She went outside, got into the car and drove to the local river, which, granted, around here wasn't a very big river, but thousands of things probably lurked beneath the surface. She found a spot off the road near the shore and reversed the car up to the edge. Then she put on gloves and opened the boot. She picked up the first bag and threw it into the black water, then a second and a third and a fourth, until she held the last one in her hands. The last part of Shaun. She swung the bag into the river and watched it slowly sink. A weight lifted of her and went down along with it.

It was like he no longer existed.

When Jane returned home, she went quietly upstairs and removed the chair from Tim's door. Then she knocked.

"Tim?" called up to Tim.

"What do you want?"

"Have you seen your father?"

"No," said Tim, clearly more bothered about being bothered from whatever he was doing.

That night Jane had no trouble sleeping. The empty bed allowed her to stretch out. When she woke up, she rolled over and pulled the phone from its holster, composed herself as a worried wife and dialled 999.

"Hello, what emergency service do you require?"

"Police please" she said.

She waited twenty seconds or so before she heard the phone being picked up.

"Hello?" she said. "I haven't seen my husband since yesterday morning and this isn't like him to go wandering off…"

The rest of the conversation went on like that, back and forth asking Shaun's routine where he may likely be, and the best bit for Jane was the information in which they told her, they would not look for a missing person until forty-eight hours after the last sighting.

Jane ran downstairs. Tim was there in the kitchen as usual eating his cereal.

"Umm, Tim, I've called the police because I haven't seen your father since yesterday and I'm scared."

He grunted and didn't look up.

"But happy birthday my lovely bunny, I love you!" she kissed Tim on the cheek. He flinched, but carried on eating.

"Thanks mum."

Jane's gaze went to the oven. The timer had wound around but still had a couple of hours left to go. "Are you excited for your birthday party today?" she asked. "I've cooked the most delicious meal for the parents."

"Great," said Tim. He finished his cereal, sighed, got up and went back upstairs.

Jane opened the oven to check on the meat. It looked great, sizzling away, just like something out of the restaurant.

She got up and started to decorate the kitchen and the backyard with banners, balloons and party poppers. She prepared salads to go with the steaks. Precisely dicing and chopping up all manners of vegetables. Time ticked away and before she knew it, lunch time came, along with Tim's friends and their parents.

The bell rang and Jane rushed to the door.

"Hey guys!" Jane gushed. "Come to the kitchen I've cooked a lot of lunch for everyone!"

Four kids pushed past her legs to wish their friend, Tim, a happy birthday. Unfamiliar adults smiled and waved, some clearly planning to drive away, but she pleaded and cajoled, dragging them all into the kitchen.

She dished out food onto plates and allocated knives and forks. Before she was done, the doorbell went again and she was back out, ushering more people inside to sample her special cooking.

"How is it?" she asked her guests

"It's so nice!"

"Lovely!"

"What a nice surprise!"

For once in her life, Jane let herself feel relieved and happy.

Over the couple hours, more people turned up and more people ate the food, and bit by bit they ate it all. Eventually, she ran out of steaks, chops, rump, sirloin, t-bone, everything. By mid afternoon, the pile was gone and by tea time, Tim's friends had all disappeared back to their homes, while the birthday boy had shaken off his sullen slouch and gone back to being the smiling child she remembered.

"Did you have a fun time Tim?" she asked as they tidied away.

"It was so fun! Thanks mum! But I'm so hungry, why didn't you let me eat? All of my friends got fed."

Jane smiled. "I'm sorry. Come on I'll take you for your first McDonald's as a birthday dinner!"

Tim flashed her a wide smile. "Thanks mum!" he said and ran out to the car.

Jane picked up her keys and just for a moment, her smile slipped. *Mcdonalds? What was I thinking?*

"Scum," she muttered under her breath. "They use processed meat."

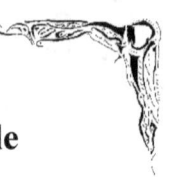

Five Kinds of People
by Allen Stroud

4.17pm at the dentists.

I hate waiting for anything, but it's worse when you know you're guilty. You've been lazy, you let things slide. You've been wasteful and neglected what you swore you'd do. After the wait, those judging eyes will be there and all you can do in the meantime is sit and practice what you're going to say.

The wait is bad; anticipating what comes after, makes it so.

"Mr Thompson to see Miss Sharp? Mr Thompson?"

A man gets up and shuffles out. I watch him go then look around the room. Me and two other people, middle distance stares all round. Old walls; the paint fading to an unhealthy yellow, a batch of magazines lying on the table and all manner of posters for self-help groups, checking yourself for lumps, diets, exercise, the works. I check the clock - 4.23pm now. This is a modern place of purgatory, complete with unidentifiable eighties cover tunes crushed out of the wall speakers. We're all waiting for Saint Peter with his scales, or in my case, Miss Sharp with her mouthwash, dental brush and drill.

I yawn and stretch, triggering the throb in my jaw that prompted the emergency appointment. Thirty-four years of age and I've never had work done, today might be the day. I'm dosed up on all the painkillers I could find, but there's only so long you can fight tooth decay with ibuprofen, codeine and salt water. Eventually, sympathy from the wife and kids runs out and you need to 'do something about it' even though you know what that'll mean. There's a child voice in my head all proud of never having been drilled and filled. I remember watching all the other kids with their 'train tracks' and metal bars, my mum scolding my sister for eating too many sweets. I get the praise and that praise becomes part of who I am; 'Mr Good Teeth', who only needs to brush once a day, yeah about that...

"Mrs Lane? Miss Sharp is ready for you now."

I read all the posters and I'm looking at the magazines for the fourth or fifth time, trying to see which one contains the least syrup; a straight fight between 'Good Family Weekly' and 'The Style People'. They are well thumbed. Could I catch something from picking them up? Can I be seen reading either, even by strangers?

God I'm bored!

These days the cool kids take their phones to places like this. They don't really wait for anything, just divert into their social lives while the rest of the world catches up. Jemma and Daniel, my two, are like that, drives me nuts when you can't get them away from those little flickering screens. Isn't life supposed to be here? All around us?

I stare at the other guy left waiting. He's older than me, unshaven and wearing a long coat. His brown grey hair is tangled and unwashed. He glances up at me. We both flinch away, pretending we didn't share a moment. People don't talk to each other when they don't know each other, but how does anyone get past that? If no-one spoke no-one would ever—

"Mr James? Miss Sharp is ready for you."

The man gets up and goes. The double doors swing closed, leaving me with the twenty year old boy on reception. That's weird. No-one's come out so far. Did I miss them walk by? I'm pretty sure not, that'd be a distraction from the wall posters, throbbing jaw and electro eight-beat.

I stare at my hands, picking the dirt from under the nails and attack a crusted stain on my jeans; probably barbecue sauce from yesterday. At least being here gives me a bit of time to think about what happened, what Helen said to me. It feels unfair. She knew I was in pain, but still chose last night to talk about separate beds. We've been together fifteen years. I never thought we'd—

"Mr Frakes?" I look up; the reception kid is leaning over his desk and glaring at me. "I called you. Weren't you listening?"

I stand up and glare back while edging my way to the doors, but I'm already forgotten as the manchild goes back to his world of social media. Apparently they call this a job? I guess if he wasn't here though...

I'm through the doors and the strip lighting flicks on automatically. I turn around; six plaques on the wall. I go right, heading for 'Miss Sharp' - the only person working here this afternoon; still no sign of any other patients or how they got out. I walk down the corridor and all the way to the end.

Three steps from her door, I hear a man screaming and I stop.

It came from inside. Where I'm going. My instincts are confused. I'm supposed to walk forward, knock, and go sit in the big chair, keeping my appointment. That's what good little citizens do.

A second scream, choked off by a gurgle. I half turn to go back and trip over my own feet, stumbling towards the door. They can't be ready for me if someone's still in the chair, but the receptionist told me to go through, there must be some—

"Come in!" says a woman's voice from inside.

I didn't knock. How did she—

"Hurry up!"

The voice is compelling, like a schoolteacher using that tone. My hand shoots out to the handle, turns it...

...the door opens.

A woman stands the other side wearing medical whites and rubber gloves. Alabaster skin, beautifully made up, ruby red lips with perfect teeth behind them. She stares at me with a pained expression. "George Frakes, yes?" she says. "I haven't got all day."

Heat builds in my face and I shuffle in as she holds the door. It thumps shut behind me and I hear the click of the lock.

"Umm. Why did you—"

"Hush now Mister Frakes, please take a seat," she's looking at a clipboard and scribbling with a pen. "By all accounts you're in a fair amount of pain?"

"Yes." I'm not really paying attention. I'm looking around the room, windows, blinds, mid-afternoon sunlight and a big purple recliner like you expect with a paper cup of coloured rinse right nearby. No sign of the screamer. In the corner there's a swivel chair on wheels and a laptop with a spreadsheet open on the screen.

She waits until my eyes finish their three-sixty appraisal and return to her. "Sounds like we may need to do some work, when was your last check up?"

"I... errr... I think I was fifteen?"

"Okay," she purses her lips and looks as if she already knew the answer. "Being here makes you nervous?"

"Well, a little, but I thought I heard—"

"What?"

"S-Screaming."

She stares at me, then smiles. "Didn't you pass Mister James in the hall on his way out?"

"No, I never saw him."

She steps forward. "Are you sure?"

I think about it. I'm pretty sure. I mean, I didn't see him, but could I have missed him? I did turn around; perhaps he got by me? Had to be, after all he's not here. She's looking at me hard and suddenly I'm not certain. Do I want this confrontation?

"I guess… maybe," I say.

Miss Sharp sighs and smiles. "Well that's settled isn't it?" She pats the recliner. "Hop on, and let's take a look at you."

I slide onto the chair and sit back. She leans over me and I catch a whiff of perfume, subtle and sweet. She's inches away, those perfect teeth making mine throb all the more.

"Open your mouth," she says.

I swallow and do as instructed, hoping there aren't any refugees from the packet of crisps I had for lunch left in the usual picking places. I know she sees teeth all the time, but suddenly I'm at a disadvantage and want to make a good impression.

"Hmmm... got here in time I think," she says. There's a tiny concentration line on her forehead. A hand spreads out on my breastbone and I feel the scraper working along the lower right side. I make my tongue as scarce as possible. Then, in comes the polisher and the vibrations in my jaw set off my throbbing teeth again.

"Owrl..." I gurgle.

"Don't be a baby, we're only getting started." The hand disappears from my chest and the polisher's gone. I sit up. "I'll need to do some work I'm afraid Mister Frakes," she tells me. "Gas or needles?"

"Excuse me?"

"I know you're nervous," Miss Sharp says. "We don't usually offer gas to adults, but it might make things easier for you."

I glance around. "Are you allowed to just... on your own?"

She laughs. "It's that or you're going home in pain."

I shake my head. "I can't cope with that."

"Well, best to go for gas I reckon." Her fingertips are on my chest again, easing me back. She pulls out a mask with a rubber hose attached. "Just breathe normally," she says as she puts it over my mouth and nose. I do that, resisting the urge to gulp in a lungful or the opposite. There's a sweet smell and taste, like her perfume...

And then the world explodes.

A burst of sunshine and it's like a bright spring morning. Brilliant yellow flowers on the shelf, how come I didn't notice them before? Growing now, growing fast, creepers spilling out onto the floor. The carpet's gone; it's fresh green grass instead. I can hear birds; smell the morning dew and Miss Sharp...

Wings unfurl on her back, flashing and translucent in the sun. She smiles and licks those perfect lips. The rubber gloves are gone and I can see her perfectly manicured hands holding the scalpel as it grows into a knife, the blade long and sharp. Her white surgical shirt dissolves into porcelain skin, the perfect line of her neck down to pendulous breasts, nipples cherry red and tempting.

"Hold still Mister Frakes," she says in a low seductive tone.

The mask falls away. I know she is naked, she's always been naked. I want to touch, to bite, to taste, but I can't. My fingers twist and reach for her, but my arms, my legs and my head won't move.

She gets up from her chair, climbs onto the recliner, a knee moves between my legs, pressing against me there. I'm hard, I can't help it. "What are you..."

"You don't remember the last time you saw me do you?" she says, whispering. Her left hand is beside my head, fingers stroking my hair. I can feel her nipples against me and the softness of her around them. "You were a child. I was quiet that night when I snuck into your room, but you saw; only you didn't believe. I rolled you off your pillow, took your little offering and gave you the silver piece, like I do for all of them." She licks her lips, blood red tongue flicking out towards me. "All grown up and lost to me, the real me, until now."

"This can't be happening," I mumble.

"Why not?" she asks and smiles again, showing me her perfect white pearls. As I stare, they grow, sharpening into little dagger points - a beautiful mouthful of fangs. "Is your life so empty that this must be a dream?"

I blink and swallow. "Things like this don't happen."

The tiny crease appears along her forehead again. "Perhaps not to you," she says and the smile fades. "But to others the world is not all microwave meals, sauce stains, social media and clock watching." She holds up the knife and smiles. She looks hungry. "Open wide for me George," she purrs. "There's a good boy."

I want to obey, although something inside me knows it is wrong.

I open my mouth.

Thirty-two little beauties.

George is still twitching, the way they sometimes do after I finish. I put down the pliers, climb off the chair and move to the sink, washing my hands and my new treasures. The blood soon disappears, leaving behind a collection of shaded jewels, ranging from cream to deep nicotine yellow.

I take the sponge from the side, wet it and begin washing myself. The water is cold on my bare chest and George's claret stains quickly spread into a faint tinge. Good enough for the street where a glamour can come undone, especially when there's lots of people about. Hiding in plain sight means practical solutions at times, not just magic.

Besides, Tobias will like the smell.

To the cupboard next, I pull out the clothes I'd taken off at the start of my shift and put them back on. I feel dirty and supressed, but it's a necessity. My wings retract and fold beneath the shirt. The cotton makes them itch, but I can bear it, at least for a short time.

I let the room glamour drop. The bloodstained walls and stack of corpses at the back of the room re-appear. It's easy to forget it all and it's important that I do. The magic won't work at all if I don't believe in it. That's how lots of other faeries lost their way.

George is still twitching as the modified dialysis machine drains the last of his juices into a big demijohn. Thankfully, I don't need to feel or look at his dick anymore, the lack of blood in the body takes care of that, but the scalpel sticking out his forehead will need pulling out and cleaning. The body will need to be disposed of with the others.

I move across the room and open the bottom draw of the filing cabinet, a pair of yellow eyes peer out at me from the darkness.

"Are you going to behave this time?"

A get a growl in response. Two furry hands grab the side of the draw and Safia leaps out onto the dirty carpet. She was beautiful once, long ago before she got trapped in this form, with these needs. I owe her, although she probably doesn't remember, stuck in a fading feral mind as she is. That's why I take care of her.

She stares at me, holding back, waiting for permission. I nod in response.

"Yes, they're all for you. Get to work."

Safia leaps on to George's trembling corpse. Her jaws clamp into the fleshy stomach. A noisy, messy gorging that makes me smile. I move around her and back to the sink, pick up the teeth and tip them into my handbag with the others. Then open the door.

"I'll be back later. Try not to make too much noise."

Safia isn't listening; she's tearing at flesh with her hands, feet and mouth. I sigh, shut the door and turn the key in the lock.

Matthew on reception has his head buried in his online social life. I slip past calling out a 'goodnight' as I do. He knows to lock up after me and being a lazy child he'll skip on checking the rooms as he always does.

I'm out of the doors and on the street as the sun is starting to fade. I keep my head down and avoid eye contact. Most of the school children are home by now, but the roads are thick with commuter traffic. Durrington is like many other dull grey modern towns, less local trade and more uncaring workaways. This is no place for people like me, like Safia, like Tobias, but we get by and that's all anyone can do.

I sit on a park bench across from the solicitors and the funeral parlour. 'White and Associates' is emblazoned on a big plaque in a font that tries to appear serious and modern without falling into drama. Being semi-attached to a coffin shop does enough to raise a wry smile from anyone passing by. Lawyers suck the life from your bones and send the remains next door.

If only they knew.

I'm hungry. I reach into my handbag, pull out one of George's teeth and pop it into my mouth. The taste brings back memories of him as a child pretending to be asleep whilst I lifted his head and took his gifts. Teeth are like trees to me. You can read a lot in the chips and scratches; a first kiss, the pain of a breakup, etc. It's all there to saviour.

But this evening I'm starving and there's plenty of George nuggets left to dwell over. I grind up the little molar with my own and swallow it down.

The sun sets and the shadows lengthen. I get up, push the traffic light button and cross. I reach the door of the funeral parlour, fish out a key from my bag, unlock the door and head inside.

The front room display is unattended and the lights are off. I make sure the closed sign is displayed and lock the door behind me. I move behind the counter and into the backroom.

Tobias' warehouse.

There's the scent of worked wood in the air. In another time, I might have considered that a sign of danger. Many of our kind took the shape of trees before they lost themselves, but there's not a lot we can do to help them now.

I flick on the light. There's a coffin in the middle of the room on iron supports. Its polished sides gleam, the brass handles are beautifully made. Any corpse would be proud of a voyage to the underworld in this pretty box.

"Tobias?" I call out.

The coffin shifts and the lid pops, sliding to one side. A man with black hair dressed in overalls sits up. He turns towards me and smiles. "Sorry I was trying out the new model," he says.

"You do that with all of them?" I ask.

"Of course." Tobias carefully levers himself out of the box. I catch sight of the cushioned padding inside. After he is out, he brushes it down a little. "I take it you're here with good news?" he asks.

"I am," I say. "Supplies secured for us both."

Tobias smiles, showing his fangs and betraying a little of his own hunger. "You smell good," he says. His eyes wander over me; such a predictable little boy, he's been doing that for decades no matter what glamour I wear. I feel sorry for him. His form's not ugly, but it must chafe, particularly with the daylight allergy and the blood hunger. He was a faery like me once, but too much time in a little village when Hammer Horror was all the rage makes people believe in things. Tobias happened to be there and get stuck. Still, at least he kept his faculties when he lost his glamour, unlike Safia.

"I'll need you to drive up this evening with the van." I tell him.

"I can do that," Tobias says. "You staying to help?"

"I can't, I've another appointment."

Jeannie, the sexy little shifter; the blood on her has me drooling. Dolled herself up before coming over here I bet.

"What about the police?" I ask.

She shrugs at me, making the good stuff jiggle. "We play it like we did before and see if they catch on. By tomorrow, this face and 'Miss Sharp' will be gone. I'll go back to pillow stealing for a while until everything settles down. You just need to pick up your share and do the last bit of tidying."

As usual with this arrangement she's left the hard stuff to me. Typical Jeannie, always good with making a mess, but never concerned with details and loose ends. "It's all right for you," I say. "You can flap your little wings and be out of here. Making a nest for me and mine takes time. I've a good thing here and no wish to lose it."

She pouts. "Don't you want all that blood?"

I sigh. She's right, of course I want it. I want her too, but that's only because she's bathed in the stuff. I know the tits and arse are all an illusion. I've no idea what she really is under it all, but then I guess she doesn't either.

Sure we've fooled around a little in the past, but she's careful to hold back. I'm not angry about that. She's kept an eye out for me and I owe her; fifty years since she found me bleeding out in a barn. I don't remember much of what went on before, but someone had been sucking on my neck something fierce and I thought I was all done.

I had a life before. I get flashes, but I can't remember it.

"All right, same deal as last time," I say.

She smirks, hands me a key and a scrap of paper. I go to the draw and pull out the last four teeth I saved from Mister Carruthers, an eighty-two year old grandfather who I measured up and boxed last week. He didn't have a full set and unlike other outlets, Jeanie doesn't take plastic.

"Pleasure doing business with you," she says.

I grunt and huff in reply. The last time we did this was out of town in some rotting little village twenty miles away. The local news had a field day with it all. Thankfully, it was far enough away for the boys in blue not to put two and two together. Profit wise, the deal works better for her than me. Each patient she gets gives her supplies for two or three weeks. I'm lucky if what I get lasts ten days and the hassle makes life difficult. At least there's no CCTV outside her surgery and where I park the van. There might be a little engine trouble to take care of first; otherwise I'm left driving a hearse.

"Okay, I'll head up there in a few hours, when it's proper dark," I tell her. "Anything else I need to worry about?"

"Only the receptionist, but he'll be long gone," she says.

"Fine."

She's gone in a moment or two, letting herself out. I yawn, stretch and make for the fridge. Half a pint of Type A positive will keep me going for tonight and sates the thirst Jeannie's kindled with her blood bathing. I have to hand it to her. Turn up just as I'm waking, smelling like a messy homicide? She was always going to get her way.

Afterwards there's business to take care of; messages on the phone from the day staff and a whole bunch of emails. Get the boring things done first. Turns out I've three new bookings and ten inquiries, plus a walk in and some spam.

Yes, even vampires get spam.

After that I'm out of the office and into the preparation room, only the one patient on the slab, Missus Checkley, due for pickup tomorrow. I check the pipes and bottles. Yep, she's ready. In my worst days, old blood like what's draining from her would be all I could hope for, but now I'm better connected. Quite a little franchise going with little deals here and there; favours in, favours out, that sort of thing.

I pick up the phone and dial. A familiar voice answers. "Glad Tidings Care?"

"Mike it's Toby, are you free tonight?"

"What do you have in mind, honey?"

I smile. "Not that I'm afraid. Jeannie's been over. She's lost it again and left me a pick up at the dentists. Interested?"

Mike sighs. "That girl will be the end of us around here. Still, I suppose it means she'll be leaving town for a bit."

"Or finding another face."

"Yeah, I suppose." Mike goes quiet for a minute. "I think I'm going to say no this time Toby, sorry. Her little hoover never leaves me enough to make things interesting."

"Nothing I can do to persuade you?"

Mike laughs. "There's always things you can do to get on my good side, but no, not tonight I'm afraid, my dance card is booked."

"Okay, shame."

The line clicks. Neither of us bothers with goodbyes, busy lives will do that to you. I don't blame Mike. He's usually pretty reliable and works at the old people's home.

Back to the warehouse and the worktable. Mrs Checkley's box is finished, but there's others to be getting on with. Two hours amongst my tools and the rest of the world fades away. It's honest work, shaping the wood; makes you feel like you're achieving something, doing good. Perhaps that's the nearest people like me get, but we're all trying to make our way in the world only the rules are a bit different for vampires, faeries, necromancers and the rest.

Quarter past eleven. I down tools and start packing the van with cleaning gear and anything else I'll need. A check under the bonnet doesn't reveal anything wrong and when I turn the key, the engine starts fine. *Weird.*

I drive around town for a bit, it's all roundabouts, electric lights and concrete. Humanity has broken free of any restraint and balance with its land. It dominates, infects and ravishes all before it. We are the monsters in books and films, yet our needs are pure and simple. We do not corrupt and poison the world around us. How are we evil? A successful vampire doesn't kill; he survives, thrives and disappears into society. We're pragmatic too; content to work with anyone who earns our trust irrespective of gender, race, species, language etc. If you can do the job, you're in. Pay your taxes, live and let live. We don't take a shit where we sleep and tell anyone different to us to fuck off back home.

I pass Saxon Supermarket, turn left into a back street and make a right at the end. The place is just up ahead; 'Durrington Dental Practice' - in the daytime, full of white middle aged, middle class masochists addicted to sugar, their rotting mouths pandered to by others trained to sit in judgement and handle gleaming metal tools. It's the inquisition repeating itself, another flagellating war against sin. Thankfully my kind gets to opt out. Something about the change affects teeth.

11.50pm and I turn into the car park; it's empty, as I hoped. I drive to the back, three-point and reverse in front of the fire escape. I get out, go to the rear of the van, open it and use Jeannie's key in the building door. There's an alarm just inside, but the code's on the paper she gave me. I tap it in before it goes off.

What makes us better than Humans? Maybe it's the blood thing? See everyone as food and you're bound to treat them as equals. There's differences, sure, but arterial and venal are differences, sheep and rat are different too.

They don't change the way you talk to your dinner.

I hear noises and look up from the computer at reception.

I should go home. I should have gone hours ago, but there's nothing to go home to. Mum will be sat in the chair still where I left her, trying to ignore the world, a bit like I'm doing here. The last thing you want to do after work is get home and work, but dishes don't wash themselves and rubbish never gets to the dustmen if someone doesn't take it out.

I know she can't help how she is, I've been there. They said I was depressed when I was fourteen. The world closes in and it's like you're on remote. Nothing you say or do affects anything so you just go through the motions. You want to care about other people, about anything, but you can't get past what's in your own head. Six years on and I've got better at coping now, but it's a daily struggle against the black dog.

I slide out from my seat. There's no-one here, the waiting room's empty, Miss Sharp went around five-thirty and it's nearly midnight now. The different chat windows, browser games and other stuff are all still calling to me, but I'm out. Whatever's bumping around down the corridor has distracted me.

What do I do? I'm not supposed to be here, but if someone's trying to break in, they aren't supposed to be here either. What could they want? We're not a shop, there's no wall safe or cash on the premises.

I stare at the phone. Call the police they tell you, but there's never a mention of what to say when you shouldn't be there yourself. Besides, it could just be the wind.

It could be...

I've got my mobile in my pocket. I could text a friend or something, but if it's nothing they'll take the piss. Maybe a quick check first? There were some thumps earlier perhaps someone left a window open?

I search around the desk for a weapon for reassurance. There's pencils and a thermos flask someone's left behind, or a fire extinguisher on the wall in the waiting room, or some magazines I could roll up? Only of use if there's a fire or a vicious wasp. I can't smell smoke, so I take a copy of 'Good Family Weekly', but leave the extinguisher. I'd need the key for it and would have to explain why I moved it, anyway.

I cross the waiting room to the surgery corridor and stop by the double doors, trying to be cautious, but the strip lighting senses me and winks on. There's more muffled noise too. Whoever's back there must know I'm here now. I could make a run for it or—

I charge through the doors, hoping the noise will startle the intruder. The fire door is open, there's no sign of it being forced and a man's standing in front of it, wearing rubber gloves and holding a mop. He looks at me and raises his eyebrows.

"Oh... Ummm..."

"Sorry, I thought there'd be no-one here," he says. "Toby Steyn, Miss Sharp called me? Told me there'd been a spillage?"

I relax and put the magazine down on a shelf. "No-one told me—"

"She probably didn't think you'd be here," Toby glances at his watch. "You're the last one on the list. I'd have been here earlier if the toy shop hadn't been playing host to a gang of upset stomachs."

I relax and stuff my hands into my pockets, feeling the two pencils I took from the desk. "Well, if you're all right, locking up after you, I guess it's okay. I'll get my things and leave you to it."

Toby shrugs. "Don't leave on my account. I'll be gone in half an hour. I could do with a quick hand though if you can spare a—"

A low growl came from beyond the door of Miss Sharp's office. We both turned towards it. "Strange," Tobias says. "You keep any pets here?"

"Not that I know of," I say. We both remain motionless, staring. Eventually I take the hint. "I suppose I should check."

Tobias holds out the mop. I walk towards him and take it. "Thanks, I'm not sure I'll need this but—"

He moves impossibly fast, pinning me to the wall, the metal shaft of the mop across my throat, his knee in my groin, his mouth against my ear. "I'm sorry, but you've seen my face. I can't have you talking about it."

I can't breathe... his eyes hold mine... I can see flickering worms of light then things start to go dark. I hear growling, louder and louder and...

Eet eet nise!

Old frend give dead peepul, tayk teeth. I do as told, kum out and eet eet eet! Then I likk up likk up gud lyke shee want. Likk likk likk so it all kleen.

Lots eet mayke me big. No fit bahk in draw.

I lyke flesh, I lyke lyke and thuh brayns best. I eet and know wurds agen. Brayns eet mayks wurds eesee kum. Betta think betta much!

Sun goes down. Old ded man kums. He stink badd and pikk up big tank of blud. I hyde and wayt. He not lyke mee.

Heer voyses owtsyde. Nutha man, yung fresh fellah. Moar meet, not bad hungree but not say no.

I sneek owt. Behind ded man, him killin yung man. I grab sqweez both togetha. Brayk brayk brayk! Flesh pulp in fingas sqweez moah! Bones bend, brayk, tayr, mash!

Lots mess! I eet eet eet and likk likk likk as she want. Fresh meet!

I think better now. Old dead man taste like dirt and rot, but new flesh throbs as I eat... everything, makes my mind clear, like fog lifted. See light go from eyes as I crunch up bones, eat more, eat all. Leave no mess.

Last stains to clean up, I lick the floor and the walls. Eat the clothes and the rest, all of it. While the flesh is wet and fresh I can think. I am large and bright. The memories come back. The shame at what I am, what I'm doing, what I must do.

I tip the glass jar into the drain and lick up the last of the blood. The fog comes back a little, but not too much. It helps;

74

some of the guilt goes away. We've all got our sins. I shut the van, tidy up the mop and bucket.

I think of Jeannie and she hears me. She is coming. She will know what to do.

I go back to room and wait. Only little thing I keep and not eat from young man. Keep for her. Leave on floor.

Leave her the teeth.

A Drop in Time
by Ben Hopkins

It was late, the skies were clear, all Fin could hear was the wind gently passing through the leaves on the big oak tree outside his living room window. A roaring fire crackled gleefully in the grate. He sat in front of it with his feet up on the small antique coffee table, eyes fixed on the book that rested in his right hand.

He heard a cupboard open in the kitchen and then close, moments later he saw his wife, Beca, in the mirror that hung above the ornate mantelpiece. She was clutching a bag of crisps in her hands. She popped her head around the door. "Just heading off to bed," she said sweetly, trying to hide the bright yellow bag of goodies.

"Don't think that I haven't seen them missy, I know your game!"

She flashed a cheeky smile and turned to climb the stairs to bed. Fin returned to his book. How could the residents of Hillside create such an infamous name for themselves? He yawned, tearing up slightly as he did. It had been another long and tiresome day at the office. Fin was a policeman; he helped out people where he could, answer the sweet old ladies who had misplaced their cats. Nothing spectacular and really not what he expected when he joined the force. He had another day in tomorrow, but the book...

He got up and meandered into the kitchen. Tea bag, hot water, nicely brewed, one sugar, a splash of milk, sorted. He took his witty, 'You're wrong, I'm right, Let's move on' mug back to the living room to revisit the world of cowboys and western frontier cliché.

He wasn't sure when the words began to blur and his eyes closed...

Now, Fin was awake, but his eyes were not. All he could see was darkness. A deep macabre he tried to challenge. There was such a depth to it. He felt as though his eyelids had been welded shut; he couldn't open them. He rubbed at them with his hands, to be rid of the rheum. Eventually, he managed to blink and focus.

Blue, that was all, and a bit of white slowly taking its time to trudge across the canvas. He sat up. Dust and mud, with the odd shrub slowly adding themselves to the scene. He looked around. A row of buildings to his right; a row of buildings to his left. The various shops and houses looked satisfyingly symmetrical, doors in the middle and windows on either side, with wooden porches slapped on the front of each.

As the glare faded, he noticed many people, still like statues, their eyes fixed on him, sitting happily in the mud.

Fin stood up and whipped away the dirt. Eager to escape the awkwardness, he hurried into the nearby building with the old cracked wooden sign bordered in red hanging loosely above the doorframe and the swinging doors between them. He pushed his way inside.

He found himself in a smoke filled room, tables scattered around the floor, some standing, some not so lucky. He heard a whistle from overhead; a woman up on a balcony backed up by a few others, just staring down at him. Two of the girls behind her giggled. Before he could even make it to the dust covered bar, the man hiding behind it exclaimed,

"Son, what do you think you're doin'? You need some clothes!"

The man whistled sharply at a girl up on the balcony. To his horror, Fin realised he had been stumbling around the town totally bare! He swiftly threw on the clothes that had been tossed down from the first floor, trying to regain some composure and dignity.

"Now what'll it be for ya?"

"I'm good for the time being thanks," Fin replied politely.

"Now look ere, you can't just come in and not get nothin', this ain't no free house."

Fin patted the clothes. "Err, you saw everything I have... I can't afford to pay."

"Then you'll have to owe me."

"You buyin' rounds for everyone, old man?"

A new voice from the door, rasping and tough. Fin turned. Standing in the door were five tall strangers. They approached the barman slowly, menacingly. Everyone else stayed still and silent, no-one moved.

"Five whiskeys on the house, now."

The barman silently did as he was told, reaching under the bar without hesitation. He laid out five shot glasses and went to fetch the bottle. He started to pour out the shots, as he went for the fifth and final glass, one of the men grabbed him and lifted him over the bar, to slam his body on the floor. The whiskey bottle hurtled through the air and smashed against a wall.

"When are they movin' it?"

"I don't know what you're talking about!" the barman screamed.

"Oh I bet you do" the man replied. "You know, and you're goin' tell me, or else..."

"Or else what?"

Fin watched the man dragged the barman across the grubby floor and onto the porch. "Or else you are goin' to have a long drink, you thirsty? Where are they moving the loot?"

"Some at dusk and the rest in the mornin', by train along the northern track! Please don't kill me Mister McCann," the barman pleaded.

"Thank you my friend, you have done us a good favour." McCann loosened his grip, allowing the barman to breathe heavily as he sat on the floor by the open doors. The man turned to Fin and looked him over, taking in his ill-fitting britches and shirt. Fin stumbled back under the scrutiny and all but fell into a chair.

McCann laughed and his companions joined in. "Always liked coming here," he said. "Always been worthwhile, but seems they'll let anyone in now an' folk have got loose with their talk. Still, dead rats don't squeak, eh?" He grabbed the barman by his neck and thrust his head into the murky water, of the horse trough under the window, laughing as he did it. The men laughed again. There was a sputtering and splashing sound, then silence.

"Ah reckon we're done," McCann said. He clapped his hands. One by one, his companions finished their drinks and trooped out.

A hand touched Fin's shoulder. He glanced up to see the woman from before gazing down at him. "You need a room and I need a barman," she said. "A position's just become available."

Fin gulped and glanced around. The bar was quickly clearing. "I'll take it," he said.

"Good. What's your name?"

"Fin."

"Pleased to meet you Fin, I'm Esmerelda. How good are you with a mop and bucket?"

"Not bad, I guess I..."

"Well, about time you got some practice in an' cleared this place up."

Fin worked all day and into the evening cleaning up the mess left by McCann and his friends, then clearing up and organising things, until Esemeralda was happy and let him down tools. The old barman, called Sam had to be laid out too. He had no family and by all accounts had just appeared in the town one morning, a bit like Fin. Esmerelda paid for his coffin. Fin got Sam's clothes and pocket watch for carrying him out and standing by while Obydiah the grave-digger put him in a hole and Father Jedda said a few words.

Fin stared at the grave. He figured he owed Sam a little. The man had tried to do him a kindness before his untimely end. He wondered what the sheriff would make of what happened? *I guess they'll be around soon to talk to us,* he thought.

Afterwards, he went back to Esmeralda's, but no sheriff arrived. Tired of waiting, Fin went out. The town was quiet. Too quiet. The people from before had vanished. The only sign of life was the horses tied up to the odd porch down the main street. With nothing else to do, Fin found himself walking around, trying to get his bearings and learn whatever he could. The place was called Sanders, he learned that from a sign. He passed the sheriff's house, but there was no-one there. He found a little market square in front of Sanders Town Hall, its clocktower cast a shadow across the mud from the evening sun.

Fin took a short stroll around the edge of the square, peering into windows and doors of the blacksmiths, the apothecary and plenty more, but no-one came out. Eventually he heard voices and people moving around. He headed in that direction, walking down a side street to the end and found a wagon being filled with what looked like solid gold bars. The building in front said 'BANK' in carved woodletters. Men were loading up the wagon, brick by brick, presumably ready to move it on to the next town.

Fin went to the door. A dark oak desk stood to the right of the room, papers spread all over it, a small chair resting just behind it slightly skewed. The walls were bare wood, apart from a singular poster hanging limply from the dry wood. 'WANTED', it said at the very top of the paper in large, black letters. The pictures beneath it were named as the members of the 'Smitty McCann Gang'. He recognised all five from the day before. highly dangerous people judging from the words 'DEAD OR ALIVE' written underneath.

"Help you son?" said a well-dressed man near the desk.

"No, just looking," said Fin.

"You just arrived?"

"Yeah."

"Well, trust me. About time you just turn around and leave." The man picked up a hat and cane from the table. Then gathered up the papers into a bound sheaf. "We about ready out there?" he yelled.

"We are Mister Matthews, sir."

"Good, then let's move," Matthews said and scowled at Fin. "They'll be one more trip after this an' then we're gone. I ain't stayin' a moment more than necessary."

Fin watched the heavy laden cart rumble away towards the sunset and the far end of town. A train could be faintly heard in the distance, getting closer with each passing moment. Fin thought about taking Matthew's advice and following them, leaving behind Sanders, Esemeralda and the Smitty McCanns.

But if I do that, how will I ever get home?

Morning came around as quick as any. Fin rolled out of Sam's old bed in the back of the bar and stretched the kinks from his back. He could hear voices outside and dressing quickly in Sam's old clothes, went straight to the door.

Crisp, clean air met his nostrils and he found people about their business in the street. Snatches of conversation came to him and quickly revealed the reason for the huddles and anxious looks.

"The town has been robbed!"

"Wait what do you mean?"

"The gold that was being taken to the next town— was taken!"

"How much did they get, do you think?"

"All of it! There is another train goin' out too! The banker folk seem to want to get the bars out before they steal it all over again!"

Fin ran towards the main street, making his way back towards Sanders Bank, but when he arrived, the whole place was locked up and shut. He doubled back, running in the direction he'd seen the wagon go the night before, but when he got to the train station, there was no sign of Matthews or a train.

Fin retraced his steps, making his way to the back of Esemeralda's hostelry. In the stable yard he found an old man sweeping up hay.

"Y'th' new fella ain't ya? what can I do ya for?"

"I need a fast horse."

The man frowned and then nodded towards the stalls. "Ah that would be the black one out back, he is a beauty."

"Yes that one, can I borrow him for a bit?"

"Well hold up now, he belongs to one of the guests. Ain't no way you can just take him off."

Fin stared at the man, but he didn't flinch. Eventually, Fin sighed and looked away. "I guess you're right," he said. "I best get back to work."

"Tha' sounds like its for the best."

"Fine, have a good day."

Fin walked out of the yard calmly, turned, and nodded to the owner before he swiftly exited. He went back to his place on the porch near the troughs and waited. Presently, the old man shuffled out and went away down the street. Fin went back the way he'd come and, checking no-one was watching, slipped into the stall old man had indicated.

The stall of the black stallion.

Oh what a beauty he was!

The horse was huge, bigger than anything he could remember riding when he was young. Back then, he'd been a child led around on a pony's back. Fin realised he had no clue how to saddle the beast, lead him out and get him moving.

I'm running out of time, he thought. *McCann's getting away and no-one else is doing anything!*

He took a step towards the horse.

Outside Sanders, Fin and the stallion galloped across dry and lifeless scrub, following the train tracks.

Fin had no idea if a horse could really catch a train. He remembered seeing things like that in films, but in real life? It didn't seem likely.

But I have to try, he thought.

The weather got worse the further away from town he rode, clouds rolled on in from the north and the wind picked up. Fin lean over the stallion and gritted his teeth. They galloped hard together, following the column of smoke from the steamer. Gradually a silver dot appeared ahead, growing larger and larger, transforming into an ugly metal beast, steaming and crawling away from him, trying to escape.

Fin urged the stallion on, in order to get to the front of the train. When he was alongside the front carriages, he grabbed onto one of the protruding ladders attached onto the side and hoisted himself up. He was a couple of cars back, still too far from the driver's cabin, but it would do. He watched the black horse slow and turn away. *Someone will find you,* he thought. *Or I'll be back soon to take you home.*

Fin gripped onto the side of the train, shimmying along the slim lip along the bottom. Smoke from the steamer now billowing into his face due to the storm like gusts of wind, he was forced to cover his face with a scarf as he yelled, trying to get the attention of the driver as he shuffled closer against the wind.

"Stop the train!"

No reply.

Fin kept shuffling forwards until he could see the driver crouched in the cabin.

"Stop this train now!"

The man turned around, surprised. "No, you don't understand!"

Fin leapt the gap. His fist caught the driver in the jaw. One swift punch and he was out cold on the coal covered floor. Fin turned his attention to the levers and dials. After a few minutes, he managed to work them out and gradually the train slowed, eventually coming to a halt in the middle of nowhere.

Happy with himself, Fin smiled and jumped off the train to the dirt. He shaded his eyes, looking back for his horse, but couldn't see it.

A handed land on his shoulder. He turned, just in time to see the baton that struck him to the ground.

The birds sang, and the wind blew blissfully through the open window of his room, just enough to stir Fin from sleep. The first thing he felt was his face, as if a fire had been started in his right cheek and jaw.

He opened his eyes to find his hands were tied with rope. He was in a very depressing looking room, dirty floorboards covered in all sorts of interesting stains; a wobbly looking table stood alone in the corner with a plate sitting on top and half a loaf of stale, crusty bread. The only thing missing from the room was one of the walls, but that had seemed to be filled in by bars.

"Afternoon, thief," grunted a man from just outside the grubby cell, sitting calmly in a chair facing the other way. "You haven't seen the devil yet, but give him my best for when ya do see him."

Fin got to his feet and walked to the bars, his knees shaking as he did so. "What do you mean? What did I do?"

"Horse theft and train robbery son, did you not realise that you were on a train?"

"Well, yes, I realise I was on a train, but I wasn't robbing it!"

The man scowled and stood up. Fin recognised him. It was the old stable sweeper from before. "You see here, how can you not be robbing a train, when you are robbing a train? It doesn't make no sense you see! No point in complainin' though, you're already getting the law's punishment."

"You're the sheriff?"

"That I am," said the man, touching the badge on his chest. "An' you're the prisoner."

The door opened. Four beefy looking gentlemen came walking into the sheriffs' office. Fin recognised them too. The men from before, who'd been with McCann. The sheriff opened the cell and they escorted Fin out into the town square, under the shadow of the clock tower. A structure had been built in the centre of it, entirely made from wood, apart from a little bit of rope tied in a very neat circle. There was a crowd too. Father Jedda, the priest from Sam's funeral stood nearby and so did the gravedigger Obydiah, leaning on his spade.

Fin knew what that meant.

"Wait! This is all a mistake! I don't belong here!"

"Maybe you're right," the sheriff said. "If so, this is the quickest way to leave."

They dragged Fin up the steps. He could feel his heart thumping in his chest. The ropes around his hands wouldn't budge no matter how hard he struggled and the men holding him were too strong. They made him kneel and rested the loop of rope around his neck.

"Do you have any last words?"

Fin looked around the square, his eyes scanning the crowd. At the back, he saw McCann on horseback sitting there, staring at him.

Esemeralda was next to him, astride a big black horse.

McCann tipped his hat, turned away and they both rode off.
The lever was pulled.
Drop.

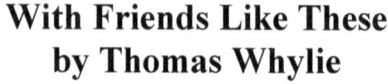

With Friends Like These
by Thomas Whylie

The world shuddered as the dragon came to ground. Under its massive frame the earth seemed frail, like glass cracking, shattering, buckling beneath the creatures's weight. On its four legs it stood, unchallenged. Its bat-like wings stretched out broader than the horizon, blotting out the sun. Its long neck swanned over, pivoting its house-sized head down towards the tiny soldiers mustering to face it. The dragon's maw gaped open, and from the abyssal blackness leading down its throat glowed a faint spark of light. Once again, the ground shook as the dragon roared with thunderous might and towards the legions of soldiers it sent a fiery tempest. The battle was over in an instant; all life within a hundred yards drowned out in a sea of dragon fire.

Alexa heard the screams, the final cries of Primlore's defenders. She was just on her way down from the mines, carrying a couple buckets of melarite ore. She had a bird's eye view over most of the city from up here and the dragon was hard to miss. This particular dragon – Pydragore the FlameReaper – would raid the kingdom on a monthly basis. The ritual was always the same. The royal guards made a stand, die and Pydragore would sly off east with the prince, princess or whatever person of royal blood it could get its claws on. Before long, a tribute of gold would be dispatched to Pydragore's lair and the hostage returned.

Most of the time.

The dragon circled the palace, speaking words that Alexa was too far away to understand, but nonetheless, they managed to convince a figure to emerge from the palace gates. One of the royals no doubt, Pydragore wouldn't have flown off with anyone else. Alexa watched the dragon go, feeling her fists clenching around the handles of the buckets she carried. Envy was starting to swell from within, a desire to be down there as one of the royal guards; to have her chance at facing the FlameReaper. If she died in service, then so what? Like all royal guards, her name would be scribed on the obsidian tablet of heroes where it would remain, immortalised for all eternity.

Her eyes remained locked on Pydragore until it became a speck in the distance. "One day," she vowed.

"Enjoying the view?"

Alexa turned to find herself surrounded by men cloaked in black. Five of them, all hooded par the one in the middle, the speaker, a man who looked to well-kept to be thug. His blonde hair, his fair skin and his green eyes suggested some breeding, though the way he scanned Alexa revealed something else. There was venom in that gaze and Alexa knew a viper when she saw one. She didn't miss the emblem on his shoulder, a demonic-looking toad stitched in white: the mark of a gang.

"What do you people want?"

The man grinned. "Please my dear, allow me to introduce myself. Arramin Vaski, chief debt collector of the Ivory Toads. You should consider yourself honoured. I am only dispatched when a debtor proves to be particularly troublesome to collect from."

"Is that supposed to be some kind of threat?"

"No," Arramin said, "but I will say this. Next time we meet, which will be soon, you and associates are going to pay what they owe, either in gold, or in blood." With the other thugs at his back, he turned away, flicking his cloak out over his shoulder.

"Assholes," Alexa muttered. She walked in the opposite direction, pacing down the crowding streets, wary of every eye that turned towards her. Slowly, people were emerging from their hiding places and life began again all around her as it always did, but she had other problems. The buckets were heavy, the sun was beating down on her tired back. She just wanted to be home; the shop around the next corner labelled 'Smoking Hot Smithies' in giant golden letters. *'We do not haggle'*, was written underneath in tiny print.

Outside by the entrance, sitting at the tanning rack by a large stone forge, Alexa saw a familiar face and mop of brown curly hair. Daeros, a name that would grace posters listing the city's petty thieves, likely declared wanted for stealing an apple or two; the price on his head never higher than a couple of copper pieces. Dareos, petty thief extraordinaire. He was dressed in a stiff leather jerkin without sleeves and didn't notice Alexa approach; he was staring at the stones in his hands.

"What's a man gotta do to get a woman around here," he said to the stones.

He paused, then spoke again in a lower pitch, replying to himself. "Change your hair maybe?"

"I've tried that Verto."

Another pause, then the voice he did was of a higher pitch, the stone in his other hand was talking, apparently. "Maybe you're just a horrible human being who will never find love?"

"Wow Astro, thanks for the confidence boost."

"Talking to your stones again I see," Alexa smiled.

Dareos looked up. "They're not stones," he said in a tired voice, "Meteorites, and they have names you know."

"Right."

"And you might want to get in there by the way," Dareos said, gesturing to the door.

"Let me guess, the guards finally came back with a search warrant?"

"Actually no, thankfully, it's Isabel. A client is trying to haggle with her."

"What?" Alexa said, dropping her buckets of ore, "And you've just been sitting out here not doing anything about it?"

"Hey, it's not my turn to be on Isabel duty," Dareos shrugged. "Besides, I plan to live past fifty. Oh and did I mention the client is also trying to seduce her?"

"For the love of all that's holy!" Alexa turned away from Dareos and headed inside.

On first glance nothing looked out of place. The mannequins were all still standing, displaying armour sets in some rather questionable poses. All the swords and maces and daggers were still hung up on the various weapon racks and no sign of a struggle. Isabel was standing by the counter, eyes trained on a nobleman dressed in finery.

"Your eyes are like rubies," the noble said, his as smooth as his looks. "Your hair, like a flowing river scarlet silk and your body? Even an hourglass would be jealous of your figure."

"How very kind of you," Isabel smiled, an eye twitching. "Now would you please pay for your order."

"I'd listen to her if I were you," Alexa said.

The man turned and held up a hand, palm outwards. "Please, ladies, let's be reasonable here." He picked up the rapier laid out on the counter. "Indeed this is a fine blade. Perhaps something could be done to cut the price?"

"How about I cut you instead?" Isabel said.

"I beg your pardon?"

"You're begging for my pardon?" Isabel growled, and without hesitating, coiled a hand around the nobleman's throat. One arm was all it took for her to lift him clean off his feet. "The only thing you'll be begging for is your life when I am ripping you apart with the jagged shards of rib cage that I am about to start pulling out of your chest."

The rapier fell out of the nobleman's hands, he was choking, barely able to word together a reply as he tried to pry open Isabel's grip. "I… just… just thought that… the price… was a little steep."

"You know what else is going to be steep?" Isabel said. "The cliff I plan to throw your corpse off from when I am done with you. Twenty silver was the agreed amount and you're going to pay in full, one way or the other."

"How about we cool off and put the pompous asshole down?"

"Alexa! Sorry about the aggressive welcoming, but this pompous asshole thinks he can just walk in here and sweet talk his way into getting whatever discount he wants on a pre-negotiated deal."

"I… I am sorry," the noble cried.

Alexa put up her hands, the same way you would to claim a spooked horse. "If you kill him then you don't get paid, Isabel. You don't want that now, do you?"

There was a moment's quiet, punctuated by the choking gargles of the noblemen. Isabel took one last look at him. "Fine," she said, then released the death grip she had around his neck. The man sank to his knees, coughing and gasping for air at Isabel's feet. "For all that is good and bloody, that's where you belong," she moaned, "pull yourself together." She grabbed the noble by the shoulders and pulled him up to his feet, the fully grown man seemingly weightless in her palms. "You don't want to be grovelling beneath me any more than I want to be beneath you. We're both human."

"Right, I-I understand, s-sorry for upsetting you," the noble said.

"Now hurry up and pay me my twenty silvers before I start restocking the leather supplies with your skin."

"O-okay, okay I-I will." Panicking, the noble dived into his pockets, counted out the payment from his purse and handed it over.

Isabel took the coins with a smile. "Thank you for your purchase, please come again."

With rapier in-hand, the noble couldn't get out of the store fast enough. Isabel took a moment to count the money herself, "Oh, he paid one silver extra, nice of him."

"Are you okay Isabel? Nothing you want to talk about?"

"I am fine. In fact, I think I'll go do some baking for a bit. Talk to you later, Lex."

"Have fun, I guess," Alexa watched with a frown as Isabel strolled away towards the staircase like nothing happened.

Dareos came in laughing, "Wow, the way that guy came bursting out, you'd think we had a dragon minding the store! Classic Isabel." He giggled to himself a while longer then hefted the buckets of ore Alexa had dropped outside onto the counter. "Heavy stuff that, how you manage to carry these with one hand goes beyond me."

"Carrying a few buckets of ore is nothing compared to royal guard initiation day," Alexa said.

Dareos leaned against the wall and smirked. "You say that like you've actually taken their trial already?"

"One day I will, and when that day comes I'll be ready."

"I still don't catch how you can be so obsessed with joining them. All they do is line up in single file to get burnt to ashes in dragon fire."

"At least they're remembered for it," Alexa said, then her expression turned sour.

"Something the matter?"

"I had a run-in with the toads on my way back, someone going by the name Arramin? Anyways they're threatening to pay us a visit."

"One of their big shots, eh?" Dareos seemed to recognise the name, "Sounds like our debt situation is about to get interesting."

"I am about to go and talk with Ignatius about it. Coming?"

"No you go ahead, I may as well mind the store until Isabel decides she wants to start working again."

"All right. Speak with you later."

Alexa took herself upstairs, walked passed the kitchen, then the bedrooms and made for the door she knew would lead into a small study space. Ignatius' study, the store's wizard, responsible for imbuing the weapons and armour forged by Isabel with magical properties.

Alexa had never been a fan of wizards or their standards. They all need to be refined, decadent, intellectual marvels. She saw them as over-privileged snobs whose wealthy families could afford to send them through the gates of Trandalore's Mage Academy rather than slum it with everyone else. *People who are more inclined to bite their silver spoon than make their own way in the world.*

Alexa knocked on the door. "Whoever you are, I'll pay you a hundred gold to fuck off," was the response she got.

"Like you have a hundred gold." Alexa cracked open the door regardless and straight away, plumes of tobacco smoke wafted out, thick enough to make her eyes water.

"Well thanks for venting out my hotbox, took ages to get it like this."

Inside, surrounded by shelves stocking hordes of books and scrolls, lurked Ignatius. He was dressed in mage robes of silvery silk scribed with runic inscriptions around the collar and sleeves. He was sat behind his desk, hood-up and feet-up. The mage's skin was wrinkled, eyes bloodshot and every strand of hair in his beard was grey, like worn iron. He was barely into his twenties.

Ignatius took a few long puffs from his pipe, then leaned back gazing at the roof. "Have you ever taken a moment to just appreciate how messed up the ceiling is?" He took another hit from his pipe. "I mean, the way it spins… makes me want to—" Before he could finish, Ignatius doubled over, vomiting into a bucket on his desk. "Damn bread."

"What the hell kind of tobacco are you smoking?" Alexa frowned.

Ignatius only smiled, "Who said I am smoking tobacco?"

Alexa just rolled her eyes. "I got the ore you wanted. There are a few things, they're important."

"Hang on," Ignatius said. "Let me straighten up." He produced a vial from his pocket and tipped some of the contents onto his desk. It was a powdery substance, blue like the sky, glowing like embers. He used a coin to arrange it all into a line.

"We need to talk about the Ivory Toads, they're coming for their money."

"Are they now?" Ignatius said before inhaling the line of powder through his nose in one breath. Immediately after, his eyes became sharper, wider and his entire body jolted as if he'd just been struck by lightning. "Ah that's the shit! Oh Alexa, honey, when did you come in?"

"I am not your honey, and I am trying to talk to you about the debt we owe."

"Right, right, right," Ignatius looked about his desk, ribbing his hands until he grabbed hold of the bucket of sick, then held it up towards Alexa. "Okay here, give this to their boss, you tell them it's from me, that it's a portrait I did of him this morning."

Alexa scowled. "For heaven's sake Ignatius, this is serious! We can't treat these guys lightly anymore."

Ignatius opened his mouth, only to close it again when Isabel came striding in. The smell of freshly baked bread followed her in, a welcome relief to the tobacco's stench. Her eyes were set on Ignatius, full of purpose; wild with passion. Without a word she walked around Alexa, carrying a tray with a loaf sitting upon it. "Here," she said, presenting her creation before Ignatius.

"Here's what?"

"A loaf of bread," Isabel smiled.

Ignatius hesitated, his eyes unsure what to settle on: Isabel or the bucket he was spitting chunks in a few moments ago. "I-I don't really want bread right now."

Isabel's smile disappeared, "That's okay, you can just take it anyway."

"I'll pass, thanks. But hey, Alexa's been mining all day, why not give it to her as a reward?"

"But I baked this for you," Isabel said, her eye twitching again.

"Well like I said Isabel, I don't want it—"

"I baked this for you!" Isabel snapped.

"Alright, alright calm down. I'll eat your damn bread." From the side-lines, Alexa smirked at the sight of Ignatius stuffing his mouth under Isabel's gaze. It was around the fifth bite when her smile returned. Overjoyed, she left without another word. Ignatius chewed until the very instant the door closed, and then he was back in the bucket again, vomiting.

Alexa couldn't help but laugh. "Good bread then?"

"Fuck no," Ignatius moaned. "Nothing that woman bloody cooks is good. And it's been going on all day like she thinks I am some kind of lab rat. She made scones for me this morning and I swear my tongue feels violated."

"Well now you know how every woman you've ever kissed feels like."

"Please," Ignatius chuckled. "You know you want a piece of this."

"About as much as I'd like a bite out of Isabel's buns," Alexa said, words that sounded so much better in her head. "T-that came out wrong."

"I am not so sure Alexa, you sounded pretty sure about yourself," Ignatius leaned over his desk. "Admit it, you've got a cock between those legs haven't you?"

If it wasn't Ignatius who'd said those words, Alexa might have started choking him then and there. What a satisfying choke it would have been too; one where you lock eyes with them and squeeze until the light drains from their eyes. *Heavens, where did that come from?* Maybe Isabel's crazy was rubbing off on her.

"Good one," was all Alexa said before turning for the door.

"What's wrong? No, come-back?"

"I have something in mind."

Alexa opened the door only a little and poked her head through the gap. Then she shouted, "Oh Isabel—"

"No!" Ignatius shot up and tried diving across the room, arm extended to cover Alexa's mouth. He didn't realise his desk was too close and ended up sliding over its surface to fall flat on face.

"I am sorry, okay?" he said from the floor.

Alexa closed the door, smiling. "Apology accepted." She stuck out a hand to help Ignatius up.

Dareos came bursting through the doorway, knocking an off-guard Alexa to the floor. "The two of you might want to get down here and... What are you two doing?"

"What?" Alexa said, and then she realised the position she'd landed in. Merrily laid on top of Ignatius. "This isn't what it looks like."

"The amount of times I've pulled that phrase out of my ass," Ignatius laughed.

"Should I come back? You two look like you need some privacy."

"Enough!" Alexa got to her feet. "Why are you up here?"

"That Arramin guy you mentioned is here. Might be a good idea to talk to him now, you know, before Isabel starts tearing into him?"

"Would that really be such a bad thing?" Ignatius said, his understanding of the situation, questionable at best. "Well I guess it would, blood has a terrible habit of staining." With pipe in hand, Ignatius got up from his desk and strolled out of the room towards the stairs.

Downstairs, the toads were waiting for them, five figures cloaked in black, the same people from earlier that day. Arramin stood in the centre of his fellows, a smug grin stretched across his face. "We are all here, my dear," he said to Alexa, "as promised."

"Sorry but we don't serve assholes. Store policy."

"What hospitality!" Arramin said. His gaze went to the wizard. "I take it you're the great Ignatius then? The first apprentice to ever drop out of the Academy."

"Wasn't my kind of scene," Ignatius puffed on his pipe. "Too many rules for my liking. Also couldn't stand for all the self-entitled pricks I was supposed to call classmates."

"And you, Alexandrea Brightwall. I understand your family used to be quite respected for a time?"

"And it will be again," Alexa said.

"If you believe so," Arramin shrugged. "Ah, Dareos. If my memory serves, you had an opportunity to join our ranks, yet you turned us down?"

"Didn't feel like a good career move."

"Indeed, because joining the crowd that's now a couple hundred gold pieces in debt is was a much better move?"

"I am terribly sorry," Ignatius turned to Dareos, a confused look about him "I did make the store policy clear, right? Why is this asshole still here?"

"Damned if I know. Maybe his parents clapped him round the head so much he lost the ability to listen."

"Please excuse my friends," Alexa said, not paying Ignatius or Dareos the attention they were seeking. "They're just playing around."

"Well I hope they understand how deep-a-grave they're digging. All of you have played a part in founding this hovel you call an establishment. Now your debtors are here to collect and if you can't pay, well, I suppose your blood will have to suffice."

"My, my," came the voice of the one person this situation didn't need. Alexa looked over her shoulder and saw Isabel, strolling down the stairs, gaze fixated on Arramin. She came over, inserting herself between the two groups and squared up to him. "Someone has guts," she said, "to just walk in here and start throwing threats. I wonder what those guts will look like when I start pulling them out."

"And in return, you believe you can threaten me?" Arramin didn't look even the slightest bit concerned, if anything he was on the verge of laughing. "No, no, no my dear that's not how this works."

"You better believe that's how this works," Isabel took another step forward, getting up close until she and Arramin were inches away from butting heads. "Now why don't you take that face of yours and get the hell out of our store before I decide to put my fist through it."

"To have the fist of such a beautiful thing like yourself inside me," Arramin said, those green eyes of his scanning Isabel up and down. "Why, it almost sounds like you're propositioning me at this point."

"Why you—"

"Now, now, Isabel let's try not to do anything rash," said Dareos, putting a hand on her shoulder.

Arramin started laughing. "I'd listen to your friend my dear, it'd be a shame for such a perfect body to get broken."

"The only thing that's gonna get broken around here is your spine!"

"Isabel!" Alexa was the one saying it this time, "Why don't you go bake something upstairs? Calm down a little bit okay? Would you do that?"

Just like with the nobleman, there was a pause, a brief moment of silence where Isabel looked at Arramin, then Alexa before finally dropping her fists. "Fine," she said, and started walking for the staircase. "But call out at the first sign of trouble."

"That's right, do as you're told," Arramin said, "good girl."

Isabel stopped in her tracks. "What did you just say?"

"I am sorry, didn't I make myself clear? I am referring to you as a dog. You know what that is right? You're the kind that likes to bark but never actually bites unless its master says so."

"A grave good sir," Dareos commented, "you've just dug yourself one."

Isabel didn't say anything more. Instead, she turned around, walked towards Arramin and kicked him in the chest. The impact sent the man flying, filled everyone's ears with the sounds of shattering rips and had Arramin smashing into the wall on the far side of the store. He held his chest, coughing up blood. He looked and pointed a finger towards Isabel, who was closing in on him again.

"Kill this—" was as far as he got before Isabel got her hands around his throat.

Alexa diverted her eyes, wishing she could do the same with her ears. The echoing screams just weren't enough to hide the sounds of ripping flesh and crunching bones.

"Oh that's just nasty," Dareos said, shaking his head; his skin going pale.

"By the gods," Ignatius said before running for the nearest bucket to vomit in.

When the screams finally died down, Alexa dared a peak. The four thugs Arramin had brought for back up were still standing in the same place, having made no move to interfere. Isabel was with Arramin's body, if you could call the mutilated remains a body. Blood was splattered all over her, and with a grip on the back of Arramin's neck, she was slamming his face into the floor over and over again.

"Isabel," Alexa said.

No reply.

"Isabel!"

"What?"

"I think he's dead."

Isabel looked at the man she was holding, his face so bludgeoned it was no longer recognisable. She took a breath and released her grip. Then her eyes turned on the other four toads. Arramin's men looked to one another, nodded consecutively then sprinted for the exit. They couldn't have gotten away faster.

"Well that was the single most disturbing thing I've ever seen," Ignatius said. He walked across the room and flipped the sign over on the door from 'open' to 'closed.' Then he turned to face everyone, "I am going to go get shit faced, who's with me?"

"Me!" Isabel said immediately.

"I second that," said Dareos.

"Wait!" Alexa said. "What about the body?"

Everyone paused and stared at her. Then simultaneously, they all turned for the stairs and started walking.

"I'll have whisky," Dareos said.

"It'll be vodka for me," Isabel said, "so much vodka."

"We can't just leave a dismembered body lying around like this," Alexa said.

Ignatius put his hands up, "I am not touching that shit. There's also store policy to consider. Whoever made the mess cleans the mess."

"Fuck," Isabel said.

"Really guys? Don't you all think this is..." Alexa paused. "You know what? Forget it. Is there any rum left?"

Everyone retired to the kitchen, a small space with a baking furnace, a round table for eating at and a cabinet full of alcohol. The sun was setting when the drinking started, aggressive and abusive, continuing onwards into the dead of night without any signs of slowing down.

"Hey Dareos," Ignatius said, offering his pipe. "Here, get a load of this."

Dareos gave it a sniff. "What's in it?"

"Just try it. Trust me it's good."

"Okay then," Dareos said as he put the pipe in his mouth. He took a few puffs then handed it back.

"Woah!"

"Good stuff right?"

"Is the ceiling supposed to be spinning like that?" Dareos leaned his chair back further, as it would assist in getting a better view, only to fall backwards off his seat completely. Everyone laughed.

"What the hell is that stuff?" Alexa asked.

"No idea. All I know is that it burns like tobacco, tastes like a manna potion and sends you on the mental trip of a life time."

"I want to try," Isabel said.

"Be my guest." Ignatius handed the pipe over, Isabel took a few puffs and everyone waited in anticipation.

"I don't feel anything."

"Really?"

"Nope, feel fine. You try it Alexa."

"Why not," Alexa shrugged, "not like this day can get any weirder."

Alexa had the pipe passed to her and was just about to take a puff when:

"Holy fuck, the ceiling!" Isabel jumped out of her seat, "what's it doing, where did all these colours come from, why do I hear a buzzing?" Tears started falling down her cheeks as she fell back into her chair, "You know what guys? I love you all so much."

"On second thought, I think I'll pass," Alexa said, handing Ignatius his pipe back.

Dareos, whilst still with his back on the floor, raised a finger. "I love you guys too."

"You know," Alexa giggled, "we're all pretty much goners at this point."

"We sure are," Ignatius nodded, "no doubt the toads are going to want our heads on sticks, guardsmen too for committing murder. Even if we evade them somehow, I expect they'll put a real big price on our heads for killing a big shot like Arramin. Big enough for every low life in the city to come sniffing around."

"Hear that Dareos, you're finally getting that sizable number on your poster you've always wanted."

"Nice, can't wait to get my ass shanked… That came out wrong."

"At this rate I am probably going to drink myself to death," Ignatius slurred. "What have you guys got in mind?"

"Like I just said," Dareos pointed out, picking himself up. "I am getting butt stabbed… and again that came out wrong."

"Isabel?"

"Going to take as many of those assholes with me."

"Hold on one moment," Alexa said, "I just got the best idea."

"Oh yeah?"

"If we're going to die, then let's do it the right way: the heroic way. Let's be remembered by this world for doing something, something nobody has ever tried before."

Isabel slumped back in her seat, eyes filled with anticipation. "Like what?"

"Let's be the first to raid Pydragore's lair."

Wonder and awe went spiralling around the table. All at once everyone seemed to understand what a feat of bravery it would be to charge head first into the one place no hero had ever dared to go. To fight any dragon on its own grounds, the very concept screamed suicide.

Ignatius offered a slow round of applause, "Alexa," he said, raising his mug. "That is the single greatest idea, I have ever heard."

"Here's to that," said Dareos, raising his mug too. "If death is to be our fate, then let's make it something that ripples through history into the next age."

"The first people who took the fight to the FlameReaper himself," said Isabel, adding her mug to the pool.

"Who died trying!" Alexa exclaimed.

"Cheers!"

After bashing their mugs together and all taking one last big drink, silence descended and was undeniably awkward.

Then Ignatius spoke up. "Does anybody know the way to Pydragore?"

The Parcel
by Gráinne C Byrne

Every five minutes for the last half hour I've heard the sound of 'a rustling in the trees' on my mobile phone. It's under my pillow, reminding me I need to get out of bed and stop continually pressing the snooze button. Finally, I open my eyes and reluctantly tear myself away from my refuge. At least the nightmares have stopped and I am sleeping a little better.

I reach over without looking, grab my glass of water that I habitually have by my bedside every night and gulp it down. Afterwards, I fight the urge to lie back and wrap myself in the duvet.

Car. Why am I thinking about the car?

I jump up. My car tax ran out ten days ago! "What time is it?" I think to myself. It's almost eleven-thirty and the local post office will be closing its doors at 12.30 for the weekend. It takes thirty minutes to walk down the hill and I am battling with my conscience on whether to drive what is now my illegal old banger. A poor old codger might get in my way, or the local bobbies might have nothing better to do than check out my bright red little heap. It looks like it's been hit with a sledgehammer several times over by someone with an axe to grind and asking to be pulled over.

I opt to drive anyway. The rebel in me gets the better of the situation, and besides, I enjoy the thrill. Another ten minutes tick by in my frantic search for the documents needed to prove my wheels are indeed able to take a spin on the local hole-ridden roads.

I pull up outside the post office and join the queue that has obviously formed just before I arrived. I wonder why I thought I'd be the only person in my town, and the world perhaps, who has woken up late with a postal emergency. How conceited I am these days! I contemplate jumping to the front of the line that only people in the United Kingdom seem to know how to shape. Instead, I make the better decision to just pop my earphones in, be a good citizen and wait my turn, whilst blasting my ear drums with banging tunes from my favourite Bhangra radio.

I stand behind an older lady like me. She is holding a large letter ready for a trip down the chute and I try to get a nose at where its going. I wonder if it's going to Pakistan. She is around the same age as my Ammi. Remembering her takes my breath for a minute and I find myself wiping away tears. The woman's hand is covering the address, so I turn my attention to the man behind me who's touching my back with his protruding gut. I wonder if he has a wife and, if so, does she still fancy him after now he's let himself go to the point of no return?

There's an Asian youth with a blue bandana tied around his head, holding a bright pink plastic bag. He looks shifty and appears nervous; his eyes are continuously glancing at the entrance to the post office as if expecting someone to walk in and join him. I wonder what's in the bag?

"Have you got any boxes?" he says loudly to the postmaster, who is busy writing up a label for an old guy who had been struggling to hold a pen and needed a hand. His voice sounds shaky with a slight pitch at the end of the sentence, as if his larynx is dry.

"You'll find them over there behind that screen mate," the postmaster replies.

The youth looks at a young woman behind him; hair pulled up into a tight knot on the top of her head and the roots needing a touch up. He indicates for her to keep his space while he moves out of the queue. As with most youths these days, he presumes that communication means a grunt and a nudge. With the bag still held tightly in his hand, he goes in search of the box. He disappears around the screen and returns a moment later, taking his rightful place again. To the left of him is an empty shelf. He gently places the bag on top of it with the box beside. I notice that the top of the bag is folded over and stuck down with black masking tape. The plastic is thick and I can't make out the contents. It looks bulky and heavy.

He's sweating into cotton cloth on his forehead. He looks uncomfortable, as if he needs to get out of there. He places the bag in the box and moves it around, trying to fit it in and clearly not knowing how.

He glances at the door again.

I can't contain the urge to poke my nose in. "Excuse me, Do you need a hand? I think you might need to pack it with bubble wrap, there's a small roll over there you can buy. Is it breakable?" I ask, pointing to some bubble wrap on a shelf.

"It's okay," he replies curtly, without looking at me and he covers the box with his arm, as if trying to hide the contents. Then, he changes his mind and cautiously lifts the box, walks over to the shelf and picks up a roll. He opens the wrapper and unfurls the plastic still holding it under his arm. He loses his grip and the box slips and hits the floor with a loud thud.

"Shit man," the boy gasps.

He looks terrified and his eyes are watering as if he is about to cry. He raises his arms out to the side anxiously.

"Shall I help you?" I say.

He ignores me and as he bends down to pick up the box, the door opens and a young Asian man walks in. He is in his twenties and with the mandatory Sunni beard adopted by most orthodox Muslim men.

"You okay, brother?" He says as he approaches the boy.

"I dropped it. Sorry man."

"You got this bro. Just get it posted, yeah? I'll be waiting outside."

"No worries man," the boy replies.

He walks back outside and the boy hastily tries to finish wrapping the parcel.

I'm still watching him, my mind forming all sorts of scenarios about what he's trying to post. Perhaps its illegal? I wonder who is friend is? I make a mental note of the house number and postcode that he is scribbling onto the address label. I can just about make out what he is writing. I type the details into my mobile phone; 107 and B23 9JP.

"Standard first class, recorded or special delivery, mate?" I hear the postmaster say.

The boy's trembling is noticeably apparent now and he almost drops the box again while trying to lift it onto the weighing machine.

"Standard," he answers.

"Are you sure? What's the value of the contents? It might be better to send it recorded mate, make sure it gets there."

"First class is good," he says.

"Okay mate, if you're sure. Pass it through here will you?" the postmaster says. He attaches the postage labels to the box. "That will be twenty-five pounds and twelve pence all together."

The boy reaches into the back pocket of his jeans and throws some notes onto the counter.

"Put it in that big grey bag over there please, mate?"

As if he cannot wait to get rid of it, the boy takes big strides and hurriedly places the parcel in the bag. It is out of his hands now, to be thrown into the back of a beaten up truck embarking on its harrowing journey. The boy still appears flustered as he walks out. My eyes follow him. Through the window I can see he is greeted by the young man. He puts his arm around his shoulder and hugs him as if congratulating him. He leads him to a parked car, opens the door and indicates for him to get in. They speed off, wheels screeching, as if the green flag has gone down at the start of the Brazilian Grand Prix.

I get the car tax and achieve what I have actually set out to do today and as soon as I am back behind the wheel, I punch the postcode into my Google Maps App. Birmingham comes up. One hour and thirty-seven minutes. Toddington Avenue.

This is ridiculous, why am I searching this address on my phone? I am letting my imagination run away with me. "Come on Aamilah, stop being silly," I say to myself and place the phone back into my handbag.

As I approach my house, I find the drive empty. Aayan isn't home from his night shift arresting chancers partaking in dodgy activities and detaining them at her majesty's pleasure. He has worked the night shift for the force for a few years now and is pretty clever at his craft. Besides, he gets first prize for how he looks in a uniform. He rarely talks about his job. Sworn to secrecy, he says. All I know is that he works for SO15, The Counter Terrorism Command. I have no idea what that involves and if I ever try to talk about it, he changes the subject and shuts me down.

We met for the first time at my cousins wedding and I asked the meaning to his name. "God's gift," he said with the sexiest smile. Love at first sight, knocked me sideways and I thanked Allah for bringing us together. Two opposite poles of a magnet, that's me and Aayan. His family is Shi'a and mine are Sunni. I had no inclination he was a copper and I presumed he was a Sunni like me. We fought long and hard to be together and lost our families in the battle. They couldn't and wouldn't accept it, meaning we had to make a hard choice. I was surprised and shocked at my parent's reaction. I mean, they don't pray, or go to the mosque and Ammi hasn't worn traditional dress for years. They are so lapsed you'd think they are Indian Christian and not Pakistani Muslim. I wonder if our baby had survived they might have changed their minds knowing they had a grandchild. Even my sister took their side.

I am so engrossed in thoughts that I am deaf to Aayan's customary cheerful greeting as he opens the front door and lets himself in. He startles me as he snatches the cup I had been washing, out of my hand and wraps his arms around my waist, pulling me close.

"You smell nice. You okay?" he says as he kisses the back of my neck.

I turn and nuzzle my face to his, enjoying the closeness. I miss him when he's working. "Hey you. Better now you're home. How was work?"

"Never mind that now," he moans softly as he gently grabs my hair and pulls me to him.

I am in no doubt of his amorous intentions and he kisses me passionately. I am distracted during our lovemaking. Lately, I have lost my usual enthusiasm for it. Thankfully, Aayan seems to be unaware.

As I lie spent, my husband happily emits sounds like he's drilling up the road outside. Thoughts of the parcel keep going around in my head. It's not drugs, too bulky. Then what is it? I wonder if I should follow it and drive up to Birmingham. If my snoring old man knew of my ridiculous idea, he would do his nut, ask if it's a wind up and draw up the papers for Splitsville, citing ridiculous behaviour as grounds for tossing his wedding ring down a drain.

I leave him to his slumber and unenthusiastically attempt some household chores, giving up more or less as soon as I've started. It's all in such a mess. Instead, I curl up on the sofa with a novel I like the look of and make an attempt to glide through the pages. It's no good, I can't focus and I sit myself at the computer and click on Google Maps again, zooming in on Toddington Avenue. The parcel would probably get there first thing Monday morning. I ponder what time I would need to set off in order to arrive at a similar time. Aayan will be at work and none the wiser. I feel guilty deceiving him.

I start at the sound of my mobile. It's Saabirah, my best friend. I let it ring until it stops. It rings again. I answer it.

"Hi, Saab."

"Where are you?"

"I'm at home," I reply.

"You're supposed to be at mine. We arranged a lunch, remember?"

"Oh, I'm so sorry I completely forgot."

"Are you okay Aami? I'm worried about you. You haven't met Baasim yet and he's two months old now. Are you avoiding me?" she says softly.

"No of course not hon. Just busy, you know."

"With what? Surely you can spare a couple of hours to have a get together."

"Oh you know. Just stuff, and before you know it, time just flies. I promise I'll get over soon. I need to buy a present anyway."

"A present doesn't matter, I have everything I need and he has more than enough toys. He just wants to meet his aunty."

"I'm sorry Saab. Give him a kiss from me and I will get over next weekend. Okay. I have to go now, I'm in the middle of cooking dinner for Aayan, he's working tonight."

"I'm sad not to be seeing you. Make sure you do get over next week. I miss you."

"I will. Promise. Bye for now."

The rest of the weekend is its usual tedious self and Aayan leaves for work at his normal time at 6pm on Sunday. As he is walking out of the door, he shouts that he will be working overtime and will be late home tomorrow. *Now is my chance.* I can follow the parcel to Toddington Avenue and be back in time for Aayan getting home. He won't suspect a thing.

Monday feels like a long wait and I set my alarm for 4am and go to bed earlier than normal. My sleep is fitful and vivid; my dreams keep me stirring. At last the alarm sounds, ending my slumber. The sun is just beginning to rise and shedding some light on the day. I get ready for my journey as if I'm on autopilot.

Once settled in my car, I type my destination into my Sat-Nav like I have done a thousand times and the Dalek voice sends me on my way. The M40 is clear and I put my foot down on the accelerator and comfortably gather speed in the fast lane. Am I insane? What am I doing? This is crazy. What if the parcel contains nothing but a game's console? Or a new kettle? What if it is something illegal? There's butterflies' in my stomach, my hands are shaking and I'm struggling to quell rising bile. I manage to keep it down.

Where did that come from? Keep focused. Just keep driving.

Just after 7:00am the Dalek tells me to stop, *or you will be exterminated.* I check out the neighbourhood a little. Curtains are still drawn. It's a typical leafy suburb, not particularly affluent or underprivileged, just normal.

I slowly drive past number 107 and look for signs of life. The house has a suggestion of well off Asian owners; gold leaf gates, huge stone lions guarding the entrance, souped-up cars in the driveway and a Rottweiler sat behind a side gate looking quite forlorn and lonely. I settle a few metres away on the opposite side of the road to wait.

The postman doesn't disappoint in arriving pretty much on the button at 7:20am. He parks his little red van almost in front of me, gets out and opens the rear door and takes out his satchel full of letters, then reaches back in and pulls out the parcel.

The object of my insanity is shining right in front of me like a light fantastic.

He decides to offload the box first and rings the doorbell. Around a minute later, the front door opens and a man wearing a long grey thobe, with a striped kufi capping his head comes down to collect.

Just as he shuts the door, a white box van with 'Royal Logistic Corps Bomb Disposal' displayed on the side of it, rolls past me and comes to rest in front of the house. Two police officers leap out of it, carrying grey cases. Close behind is a patrol wagon and before the driver has time to put on his breaks, a small army of armed Old Bill pour out of the back door. In precise coordination, they surround the house and point their guns at every possible escape. As this happens, three officers kick in the front door in and storm inside. There's shouting and screams. It feels surreal, as if I'm at the flicks watching a movie in slow motion.

One of the men moves towards the door. There's something about him... I cup my hand to my mouth and gasp. It's Aayan! I frantically get out of the car and start running towards the house.

"Aayan. Don't go in there!" I scream.

He looks up and stares, taken aback. Surprise fades back into a professional grimace. His eyes urge the driver of the wagon to get me off the road.

I realise I am not breathing and gulp for air. There is no life from the surrounding houses, no faces against windows or twitching curtains. At that moment, someone grabs me in a bear hug and almost carries me towards a police car parked a little further down the road. He opens the door and puts me in the back. Tickling my face with his breath, he reaches over my lap and presses the buckle on my seatbelt.

"Please calm down miss, I need to get you to safety," he says. It's a reassuring voice, reminding me of where I am.

"Can I get my handbag?" I stupidly ask.

"Afraid not," he replies. "What are you doing here? What's your name?"

"My husband is Aayan Qureshi. He's a police officer. Please get him away from that house... The parcel... he could die. Please?"

The car starts moving and I'm hysterical as Toddington Avenue quickly disappears from view. Information and instructions calling from the radio prevent me from asking any questions on the journey to the station in Birmingham. It feels like all eyes are on me as I am led through a noisy office and into a waiting room. I collapse onto a large brown leather sofa. I am made comfortable and given a blanket. A much-needed cup of steaming hot tea is placed into my trembling hands and it soothes me a little. I put my rescuer in the picture of the whole story of events since Saturday and resign myself to a tortuous wait to know if my husband is safe.

My nails are almost bitten to the quick and I am tied up in knots by the time news of the raid reaches my ears. I am told Aayan is okay. The job has finished and was successful.

"Praise be to Allah for letting Aayan return to me safe." I sob and close my eyes, giving in to relief and exhaustion and doze off. I wake to a gentle shake from a female police officer.

"Aayan is here. He won't be long," she says.

I hear him coming. He stops in the doorway and runs his hand through his thick black hair. Our eyes lock and I stand to walk towards him, suddenly feeling weak and vulnerable. I stumble and he grabs hold of me before I collapse to the floor. He holds me in his arms until I am steady again. We sit down and face each other.

"You could have been killed," I say.

"I could have been killed Aamilah? What about you? What the hell were you thinking?" he replies.

"I had a feeling about that parcel. I saw them posting it. I knew it was dodgy. I knew they were up to something."

"It's my job to chase dodgy parcels. You put yourself and me in danger. One little mistake outside that house and we both wouldn't be sitting here now."

"I wish I wasn't," I answer sarcastically.

"What? What do you mean? For God sake Aamilah, what are you saying?"

"I had no idea just how dangerous your job is until today. You never talk about it. I'd rather die than wait for a knock on the door from the police, telling me that you are gone."

He puts his head in his hands and takes a deep breath. "It's what I do. Someone has to do it. I can't talk about it and you know that. Every job I work on is highly sensitive. One little leak and it's all over. I know you worry. I'm sorry."

"No, I'm sorry. I was so stupid," I whisper, looking at the floor in shame.

He moves closer to me and takes my hand, looks at me earnestly and says. "This isn't about my job, is it?"

"I don't know." I shrug.

"You haven't been right since the miscarriage. I kept thinking you'd get better. Oh honey, I should have taken more care of you."

I can feel goose bumps over my entire body and my heart is beating hard. The loneliness hits me again. I miss my Ammi and my Papa, my sister, my family.

"I'm alright. I've just been stupid that's all. I'll get back to work soon, honest," I say.

He is crying. I have never seen him cry before. The pulse of my heart is pounding and it feels like it's reached my mouth it's so strong. My head is about to explode and I can't move to comfort him.

"Our family disowning us, the baby, Sabiraah having Baasim, all of it. My God, no wonder you lost it," he says through wracking sobs. He drops to his knees and lays his head on my lap. There are wet beads appearing on my skirt as he cries.

An wave of sensation erupts from the tips of my toes, traveling up to my eyes just as the tears come too. I wail and weep for what feels like years of pain and loss. My husband holds me tight and we share our grief and sorrow until we have no tears left to cry.

"We will get over this. We will have a family of our own, Aamilah. Everything will be all right, I promise. I love you."

I look at my Aayan, my love, and I know in that moment that it will.

The Last Day
by Laura Bonfield

The light of the sun is burning my eyes, the blue sky glows bright. I hear a gentle whooshing all around and feel the soft grass beneath me.

I remember waking up this morning and feeling oddly content, despite the weird dream I'd had the night before. I'd been flying again, through the same starry sky as always; although this time the colours of dawn were painted across the horizon. Usually in these dreams, I'd be feeling heartbreakingly sad, but last night there was only a palpable calm. It was a strange but pleasant sensation. Something told me that I wouldn't have to worry about those night terrors anymore.

Bird have started singing amidst the noise of the wind. I reach my hand up and clutch at nothing, as if I still had the determination to hold onto something to keep me alive, something that isn't and never will be there. I gave up on that hopeless wish weeks ago. I close my eyes and open them again, in slow succession, taking in the reality of right now and absorbing the peacefulness of it all.

I wonder if she'll show up today?

Memories flicker through my mind like the pages of a book. I smile as I look back, comparing the world back then to the world now. All good things come to an end.

It was the summer after my eighth birthday, the summer before my whole world was flipped upside down. One day, my mum decided to take us all out on a picnic, to celebrate the fact that I had somehow survived an extremely risky operation on my lungs that was done to help me cope better with my long term breathing problems. I remember feeling so elated that I was finally going to be able to run around in wide open spaces again, without having to worry about suffering another asthma attack. My mood continued to brighten when I scrambled out of the car into the sunlight, gazing at the sky and taking in the wonders of nature around me. I had always been an outdoorsy kind of girl. Even now, when I am slowly fading away.

I smile as I recall the moment when my best friend Lily arrived. Lily, the twin I've never had, the one person I have the most in common with. We are connected over our shared love of life and all things creative. Our grief over the loss of loved ones far back in our childhood and the fact that the two of us have always had weak constitutions also unifies us.

I remember how she hurried over to me. I grabbed her hand and we both took off in the direction of the woods, paying no attention to the shouts of *"be careful"* behind us. We both laughed as our hair blew about in the air, long strands of my chocolate brown and her fiery red swishing everywhere. I like to think that my eyes were glimmering emeralds that day, the sparkling green of them illuminating the world around me and sharpening even the most insignificant details, into a clearer focus than usual.

But the best part of the entire day, out of all the fun and games we played, was when Lily and I found the rope swing hanging obediently over the rippling river.

I remember trying it for the first time and being overwhelmed by the sheer thrill. I felt like I was flying, up, up and up. Into the sky and away from the world below, into a place only I can see. It was one of the few times where I have truly felt alive.

Oh how times have changed.

That's all gone now. I let the memory float away and focus on the empty wheelchair a few feet away from me. It is dull and ugly compared to everything else. I glare at it, willing the thing to spontaneously combust in front of my eyes, but to no avail. I hate that I have to use this thing to get around now, that I'm so pathetically weak I can barely get out of bed anymore. No wonder she hasn't been to visit me lately. That thought only bugs me more. I really hope she comes.

A familiar stroking sensation soothes me. I raise my eyes and see Mum running her hand through my short and choppy hair. Her silvery-blue eyes are shining and her curls tickle my face as she leans over me with a sad smile on her face. My heart clenches with what strength it has left at the thought of what she has been through, particularly for me. At the age of nineteen, she married my dad and had Louise and Matthew, followed on by myself four years later and Willow a few years after that.

Yet somehow she's managed to pull through, despite my continuous health problems throughout all of my fifteen years and losing my dad just after Willow's first birthday. It was so long ago now, yet I can still recall the night the police came to our door. There had been a really bad storm the night before and there was a lot damage done to roads, cars, houses and anyone caught up in it. I remember looking out my window that night, in awe of what nature could do. The lightning reminded me of giant, spindly hands. There were times where I even wanted to hold onto those hands and get taken away into the sky. I always believed that the stars were sad that they couldn't come down and play with us. The thunder and the wind made think that the Gods were having a party up in the heavens. I was jealous that I couldn't go up and join them.

Ah, the wonders of a child's mind!

I remember sitting in a little camp made up of blankets and pillows on the living room floor with my siblings, listening to Mum read us a bedtime story when the knocking sound drew our attention away. I think back to being alarmed at the look of surprise on her face, since I'd never seen her look like that before.

"You wait here, kids. I'll be back in a minute," she said before leaving. Sticking to my usual strategy of not listening to anyone, I followed her.

Mum smiled and rolled her eyes when she noticed, picked me up and opened the door. Seeing the two policemen standing there caught her off guard and to be honest, I focused on that more than on what the officers were saying. It was only when I heard the words "husband" and "dead" that I started listening. Being five years old at the time, I only had a vague idea as to what death was. Even before my terminal diagnosis, I remember doctors and nurses talking about it whenever I'd had to go to hospital. But from what I was told, I knew that it was a very, very long sleep that people didn't wake up from. Hearing that my dad had fallen into that sleep sent shockwaves through me.

I'd always thought parents were invincible, that nothing would ever happen to them. Hearing that my dad was gone, that he'd never come back, hurt so much. I remember not wanting to believe it.

Even now, when I'm on the verge of dying myself, the grief gets to me. It strikes me like a thief in the night. It's worse now that I truly understand the meaning of death. I know why Lily's been acting so distant. She's still recovering from her mother's disappearance a few years ago and I don't think she could bear to lose anyone else. I think of all my loved ones and my heart aches. I can't leave them like this.

Oh God, I don't want to leave them. I don't want to leave them behind. It's not fair! It's not fair! It's not fair!

Mum strokes a stray strand away from my face and I relax. My hair never used to be so short. I remember having it fall to the middle of my back up until recently. I push that aside and focus on something else. One last addition to the list of things I want to do before I die.

"Mum?" I say.

"Yes, sweetie," she says.

"I want to go to the beach."

A smile appears on her face as if she had known this was coming. "Of course."

She calls over Matthew to help me into the wheelchair and as I sit down I hear screaming. I see my littlest sister, Willow, standing nearby with tears streaming down her face.

"You can't go there yet, Cass! Not now, it's too soon! Please don't leave me!" She's clutching onto Louise's arms at this point and I watch on helplessly as Mum tries to comfort her. Thank God those two are home from university for the summer; it will make this situation a little easier to deal with.

"You promised me that it wasn't time yet! You promised me you wouldn't go today!" She's sobbing hysterically, and it's then I remember the promise. The promise to Willow that I wouldn't go back down to the beach unless I was sure I was about to die. It was a secret kept between the two of us and just as it looks like everything will escalate into a train wreck, I have an idea.

"It's alright, Willow," I say. "It's just such a beautiful day that I thought we could all go down and play together."

She perks up. "Really?" She flashes me a watery grin. "Then let's go!"

I laugh at her enthusiasm as Mum begins wheeling me out of the park.

"Come on everyone!"

I continue to smile as we travel, glancing everywhere. We pass the bubbling fountain nearby and the water is so beautifully clear that it warms me inside. The grass is like glittering gems and I feel the urge to run my hands and feet through it. Behind me, there are a variety of sounds occurring and I strain my ears to listen. Music, laughter, the chatter of people, even the little sounds such as the tapping of feet and scraping of chairs in nearby restaurants are appealing to me. I capture the echo of their sounds into my head and savour the memory. Everything seems clearer today. I gaze at the rainbow painted confectionary café, remembering a good many days spent there mucking about with my friends, eating ice cream and pretty much everything else they sold. The town library passes by too, and the shopping centre and the cinema. Suddenly I find myself being caught up in a whirl wind of recollections, dreams and real life, giggling as I flick through my internal scrapbook.

I'm startled out of my thoughts when a voice calls out my name. I look, barely acknowledging the fact that we'd arrived at the beach, to see Lily, the person I was beginning to think I wouldn't see again, standing in front of me. Her flaming locks are blazing in the golden sunshine and her sapphire eyes are staring; today it looks like there are stars shining in them. Relief floods me and my eyes fill up with joyful tears.

"'Sup, Lil," I say, holding out my trembling hand to initiate our usual handshake. She looks surprised, as if not expecting me to pretend our brief separation over the past few weeks never happened. But it's not long until her famous smile is back on her face, albeit more watery than I was anticipating.

"Hey you," she replies, taking my hand. "I got your message and also, I want to apologise. I'm sorry for the way I've acted recently. It was selfish and horrible and I can't believe I let the past affect our friendship. You'll always be one of the most precious people in my life. Can you forgive me, and let me go down to the beach with you?"

I grip her hand and face the beach, ignoring the pain in my chest.

"Course I can, I'll always forgive you. And don't worry about it, I understand. More than anyone. Shall we be off?" I smile.

It's a struggle to get the wheelchair onto the sand but eventually I'm sitting halfway between the land and sea. Perfect. Now to finally get on with what I need to do. But first...

"Hey," I face my younger sibling. "You remember the rock pools I showed you a while ago, the ones that looked like they were made of crystals when the sun shone on them in the right way?"

She nods.

"Well I'm sure Matthew and Louise won't mind taking you down to explore them. You might not have any buckets to collect stuff but I'm sure it will still be a whole lot of fun." I look to the others as the little ones begin chattering excitedly. Matt has a strange look in his eye; I think he knows what's really going on.

"Well you heard the woman," Louise says grinning. "Let's go!"

As Willow bounds off with Louise in tow, Matt hugs me tightly. I smooth down his gelled hair and rub his back.

"Take care."

I can feel him shaking.

"I should be telling you that," he says, standing up. He gives me one last pat on the head and races off down the sandy path with the others. Let them go.

"Goodbye Matt," I call softly, "goodbye all of you."

The pain in my chest is getting worse and it's becoming more difficult to breathe. I have to hurry.

I look up at Mum and Lily and notice their stares.

"Say, could you take my shoes off?" I ask, "I want to go down to the sea."

My best friend quickly slides them off and my mum reaches for the handles of the vehicle.

"No, not like this," I say, "I want to walk."

Mum's face lights up with alarm while Lily looks confused. But then it dawns on them and their expressions develop into sad, knowing smiles.

"Thanks," I smile. "Now go stand at the water's edge."

They do as they're told. I place my hands on the armrests and slowly get to my feet. I keep my grip tight; I know I'll only fall if I let go right away.

"Don't push yourself too hard!" Mum cries out.

"I'll be fine!" I beam, and lower one foot into the golden sand. It's so hot, oh so very hot! Easing the other down, I let go of the contraption with one hand. It unsteadies me a bit, but I'm still upright. I look to where they stand by the sea. The reflection rising off it in the background only makes the stunning scenery even more so and it increases my focus on the goal ahead. I take the other hand off and tumble to the ground. Mum and Lily are yelling in the background but my hearing's started to go funny so I can't tell what they're saying.

I get up and successfully remain standing unaided. I have to do this, one step at a time. It takes a while but I finally manage the first one. After that, it's as if I have been allowed a brief moment to be normal. To be an ordinary girl walking along the beach.

I hold my arms out to retain some sort of balance. The others are shouting encouragement to me, but the closer I get to them, the more difficult it becomes. My vision's beginning to blur, my hearing is getting worse and I can't seem to get enough air to flow into my lungs. I don't let that stop me. I think of my life and how I've loved it so, despite the hardships. I open my scrapbook of memories again, but this time I take the recollections and scatter them to the wind like leaves. Let it all go.

The ground is damp and I know I've nearly reached my destination.

"You know, I really have loved being alive. Especially since I've experienced everything I wanted to," I say, breathing shallowly, "but I think my story is over now, and I'm okay with that."

I don't understand the replies. Instead, I feel the warm breeze blow my summer dress about and the cold ocean caress me at long last. That's when it ends.

I can barely see, it's all a giant, colourful blur. It's like I'm feeling and not feeling everything at once. It's a wonderful comfort.

"I love you," is the last thing I say with my final breath and I fall into an abyss of stars.

I wish eternal happiness for you all.
Goodbye.

I'm Yours
by Sophie Dale

Come on and chime in,
Combine this gentle sin.
Let this be more than,
Goosebumps on my skin.

Every time I catch a glimpse
I'm yours.
I die a little more.
I'm still yours.

Intoxication is a burden,
A stolen moment,
That'll never be enough.
I'll remain broken.

Why can't we touch?
I'm yours.
My love is homeless,
I'm still yours.

When you're with her,
Is it the same?
I'll sit at home
And watch this dying flame.

Hold me in the dark.
I'm yours.
A siren call of old habits.
I'm still yours.

No-one knows.
I don't want us to hide.

Why can't I say I'm in love?
Is it still your pride?

I'm in too deep,
I'm yours.
This is hopeless.
I'm still yours.

Hope is a dangerous thing,
A game of lies,
And hurt and pain, yet none at all.
Axis and allies.

You talk with no words.
I'm yours.
A warrior with no clue.
I'm still yours.

It's the worst kind of pain I know,
Anguish and patience,
Are the only company,
To my natural defence.

But you have a hold.
I'm yours.
Come close and listen hard.
There's nothing left to say,
But I'm still yours.

A Collection of Poetry
by Gráinne C. Byrne

She is the Flower

She sees him, she wants him,
Her excitement dances around her senses,
He can smell her, he can taste her,
He cannot see her,
A gentle touch, he turns,
Her beauty captivating, enticing,
Her fragrance never to forget,
A world of forbidden fruits,
It enfolds him in its love, it swallows him,
He is lost inside of her forever.

As the Sun Meets the Sea

(Inspired by and dedicated to, Yuliia Skrynska)
I feel the sand between my toes,
The breeze gently blows away my woes,
As the fire meets the sea,
It shines upon me,
And warms my soul in its flames,
The waves they whisper in my ear,
Please come float in here,
They speak of beauty, of love, of peace,
If we all looked to the sun as it meets the sea,
We may just begin to foresee,
The power to take away all our sorrow,
And pave the path for a brighter tomorrow.

Peace

They sit in the silence,
Peaceful, quiet, serene,
Sunshine peaks through the window,
A soft breeze gently caresses their face,
No pressure to talk,
No pressure to listen,
Slowly breathing in the space,
That is all their own for now,
No time, no hurry,
They are almost dreaming,
They are content,
They are happy,
They are blissful.

My Mid Autumn Day

Buzzing of bees waking up to a Spring day,
In mid Autumn,
Barrels of hay in the afternoon haze of an Indian summer
sunshine,
A warm breeze caresses my hair around my face,
I rest my soul against a tree and lose myself in the gentle
quietness,
A kestrel contemplates to fill himself, Ready to strike at
any moment,
Smoke rises in the distance,
Enfolding the landscape in its white fog,
I close my eyes to feel the beauty wrap me in its arms,
And hold me in its dream.

Summer Solstice

Driving to chase the sunrise,
Watching the moon through the corner of my eye,
Winking at the light beginning to shine,
Running to catch the fire behind the horizon,
A druid priest raises his offerings,

Opening his heart to a brand new day,
Summer is just moments away,
It rises, it shines,
It fills your senses,
new hopes, new dreams, new joys,
Just happy to be alive within our beautiful earth.

The Fire

Flickering arms and deep conversation,
Embracing the warmth in its flames,
Dancing to the rhythm of sounds,
Clouds beckoning the stars,
To capture the rapture that enfolds,
Happiness within hearts and minds,
Words with lightness that know no ending,
Candles, sofas, fluorescent colour,
Happy Birthday they say,
A party,
A fire.

My Warrior

(Dedicated to my sister, Kim)

It took a hold of her with its hot smouldering tar,
Its desire to burst away from its cage within her,
She battled it with weapons of love and poison that had no
end,
It couldn't see a light through the prison it was in,
She looked into its evil eyes and threw away the key,
To let it die a painful death,
We are of the same blood,
Strength running through our veins,
Yet she is stronger in the face of long drawn battles and
fallen swords,
She is beautiful,
She is love,
She is my warrior.

A Collection of Poetry
by Samuel Long

A Friend

Hey it's okay,
I know times are tough,
But I'm here for you, starting today,
And you might cry and wish this all would end,
But I'll be with you, every step of the way.
So take a seat, I'll be right by your side.
- A Friend.

For those without God:

If I have no God to turn to,
I'll plead with anyone that be,
Friends, partners, family,
To fix what's broken; black and blue,
And make me whole and happy.
I may not find a hopeful prayer,
To save me from this blight.
But as long as those I love surround me,
I will be alright.

For those with God:

He will stand there by your side,
Ready to support you.
And though you may not see him as you walk,
His footsteps are close by.
He will guide you from dark to light.
When he stands above,
He'll pull you to your feet,
For God will stand beside you,
And everything will be alright.

I am a Writer and I am in Pain.

A writer in pain is a tragic thing,
It dulls the hands and the pen,
And its elegant brushstrokes,
Turn art into hard and harsh lines.
Crossing the gaps between words,
With seas of ink,
That poetic flare buried,
Under black stains, forever lost.
A writer in pain is blind,
Our eyes lose sight of what inspires us,
Found in the cracks that break apart,
The mundane canvas of everyday life,
Like the red sea.

A writer in pain is lonely,
Trapped in the prison of our head,
With a cellmate as a critic,
Using your voice as a knife,
Stabbing hole after hole in your work and watching it
bleed,
Ink.
I am a writer and I am in pain.

Blocked

Ideas,

Flow like water.
Controlled by pipe like fingers.
On to the keys.
Until something gets blocked.
And the pipes run dry.

White words on white paper,
That only I can see,
My mind is locked, the pipes are blocked,
Preventing.

Ideas,
Stalled in sludge,
The words are stuck,
The ink is dry,
Nothing flowing from the pipes until.

I find the fragments of a story,
In everything I see.
My eyes will glow as the pipes flow with,
Glorious ideas.

Flow like water,
Through the pipes,
Droplets first, then a torrent,
Erupts from the pipe-like fingers,
This blank desert,
Is now an ocean.

At Least For A While
by Rory Kenny

Summer days spent on the field,
As the sun beats down on you.
Shining glory across the plain,
The bugs that crawl you show disdain.
Because everything is perfect, at least for a while.

Find solace in memories,
The good and the bad.
Remember promises and dreams,
As they unravel and entwine.
Forgotten nights with friends,
Over two glasses of wine.
Because everything is perfect, at least for a while.

Look back into the past,
Look forward into the future.
Nothing ever lasts.
Times will always change,
Turn back the clock.
Because everything is perfect, at least for a while.

They knew very well what they loved,
In times of turmoil it was each other.
Held on for dear life,
Who else was better than your wife.
Because everything is perfect, at least for a while.

About the Authors

Laura Bonfield

Laura Bonfield is a student at Buckinghamshire New University on the Creative Writing for Publication course, with a particular preference to fantasy fiction. She will write in any genre, but for the most part, her work is always set in the same faraway world that she made up as a child.

Gráinne C Byrne

Gráinne C Byrne (Aka Norny Byrne) is a student at Bucks New University studying for a BA (Hons) in Creative Writing for Publication. She likes to write music reviews and her poetry is inspired by her own photography on Instagram. She is currently working on a series of stories for autistic children and wants to write plays for radio and the stage.

Sophie Dale

Sophie is a current student at Bucks New University, High Wycombe. She studies Creative Writing for Publication and blogs in her spare time.

Suzanne Harbour

Suzanne is a student at Bucks New University, studying for a degree in Creative Writing for Publication. She loves writing anything from short stories to novels and has a particular passion for writing for young adults.

She is a ferocious reader, losing herself in books of any genre.

P.T. Holmes

Tracey Holmes is a student at Buckinghamshire New University, High Wycombe. She is currently doing a degree in Creative Writing for Publication. She enjoys reading and writing horror and poetry.

She has written book reviews for www.concatenation.org and https://sfbook.com.

In her spare time she writes on her blog www.notjustprettywords.blogspot.co.uk.

Ben Hopkins

Ben is attending Bucks New University as part of the Creative Writing for Publication Course. He likes to blog, read War Novels and create Historical Fiction when he gets the chance.

Rory Kenny

Rory is currently studying Creative Writing for Publication. Writing a whole manner of things. Focusing on songs, poems and script writing.

Samuel Long

Samuel Long is currently studying Creative Writing for Publication at Bucks New University. Samuel Long is known for his grit, descrption, and imagination in his writing. He is always trying to find new ways to suck his readers into his work. An avid fan of fantasy and science fiction, he attempts to recreate the same feeling he feels losing himself in other writer's worlds.

Allen Stroud

Allen Stroud is a University Lecturer at Buckinghamshire New University in High Wycombe, England. He runs the BA (Hons) Creative Writing for Publication degree and is studying for his doctorate in Creative Writing.

His website is here: http://www.allenstroud.com.

Allen edits children's stories for his father Geoffrey - *The Adventures of Ozzy the Pig*, which you can also find on Amazon.

Thomas Whylie

Tom is just a guy who likes writing about dragons, maybe a little too much. He studies at Buckinghamshire new university in high Wycombe. On the internet this author goes by the name Memoriator, who posts work on Wattpad, fanfiction.net and deviantart.

Should you want to know more about the BA (Hons) Creative Writing for Publication course at Buckinghamshire New University, please contact course leader, Allen Stroud – allen.stroud@bucks.ac.uk